Simon slid the band of sapphires and diamonds onto her third finger.

His fingers tightened around hers. "Do you really like the ring, Polly?"

He sounded as if he actually cared whether she did or not. "Yes." Polly made herself meet his eyes. "Yes, I do."

"In that case, it's yours for the next two weeks."

Just for two weeks. Polly looked down at the ring and was conscious of a ridiculous sense of wistfulness. What would it be like if they were here for real, not because it was convenient to pretend to be engaged, but because they were in love and wanted it to be forever?

There was no point wondering that, though. Simon was never likely to be in love with her. She was too messy, he was too precise. She was too casual, he was too organized. They would drive each other up the wall....

Jessica Hart had a haphazard career before she began writing to finance a degree in history. Her experience ranged from waitress, theater production assistant and outback cook to newsdesk secretary, expedition assistant and English teacher, and she has worked in countries as different as France and Indonesia, Australia and Cameroon. She now lives in the north of England, where her hobbies are limited to eating and drinking and traveling when she can, preferably to places where she'll find good food, or desert or tropical rain.

Books by Jessica Hart

HARLEQUIN ROMANCE®
3511—BIRTHDAY BRIDE
3544—TEMPORARY ENGAGEMENT
3581—KISSING SANTA
3594—OUTBACK HUSBAND

THE CONVENIENT FIANCÉE

Jessica Hart

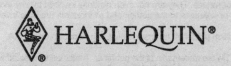

HARLEQUIN®

TORONTO • NEW YORK • LONDON
AMSTERDAM • PARIS • SYDNEY • HAMBURG
STOCKHOLM • ATHENS • TOKYO • MILAN • MADRID
PRAGUE • WARSAW • BUDAPEST • AUCKLAND

ISBN 0-373-17483-7

THE CONVENIENT FIANCÉE

First North American Publication 2000.

CHAPTER ONE

THE party was in full swing when the doorbell went again. Polly, manoeuvring her way around the room towards Philippe, was just wondering if she could pretend that she hadn't heard it when Martine Sterne snapped her fingers imperiously in front of her face.

'Polly! Go and open the door at once!'

Suppressing a sigh, Polly turned and made her way back through the crowds towards the hall. The job had sounded so promising when she had answered the advertisement, but if she had known that three months in the South of France as general assistant to a Hollywood director meant being dogsbody to his impossible French wife, she would never have taken it.

When Polly thought of how thrilled she had been when Rushford Sterne had offered her the job, and how she had boasted to her friends and family about the glamorous, exciting time she was going to have, she could only shake her head at her own foolishness.

Still, it wasn't all bad. Polly tried to be positive as she set the tray down on the hall table and straightened her cap in the mirror for the umpteenth time. Martine Sterne might be a nightmare employer who made her wear a cap and frilly apron to hand out drinks, but she had a brother whom Polly had fallen in love with the moment she had laid eyes on him.

Philippe was the kind of man she had thought only existed in movies. He was tall and lithe, with dark hair, deliciously dark brown come-to-bed eyes and a smile that made her go weak at the knees. Unlike his sister, he treated Polly like a human being, and his visits to the house were the one thing that had kept her going over the last six weeks.

She had been so looking forward to seeing him this evening, and in his honour had worn her special party shoes that drew attention to her long, slender legs that were her best asset, but she might as well not have bothered, Polly thought as she regarded her reflection with a sigh. Shoes or no shoes, Philippe wasn't going to notice her in this stupid maid's outfit!

Not that he was likely to pay her any attention, anyway. There was nothing wrong with her face, and, since she had had it streaked, the blonde hair went nicely with her blue eyes, but she was never going to win any beauty contest, especially not compared to all those ferociously slim and intimidatingly elegant women vying for his attention in the other room. Polly felt enormous next to them. She just wasn't built to be skinny, and something about her generous curves and tumble of hair made her look a mess whatever she was wearing.

It looked as if she was going to have to carry on adoring him from afar, and in the meantime, she might as well have worn some sensible shoes. Her feet were agony already.

The doorbell rang again impatiently.

'I'm coming, I'm coming,' Polly muttered as she gave her cap a final pat into place.

Wincing as the shoes pinched her toes, she fixed on a brightly welcoming smile and opened the door. On the doorstep stood an austere-looking man of about thirty with a cool, intelligent face and ironic grey eyes.

Polly's smile was wiped off her face as she stared in astonishment.

'Simon!' She shook her head as if to clear it. Simon Taverner couldn't possibly be standing on the Sternes' doorstep! He looked momentarily disconcerted at the sight of her, too, so much so that she wondered if she was hallucinating. 'Simon?' she said again, more doubtfully this time.

'Hello, Polly.'

Oh, yes, it was definitely Simon. Only Simon had that infuriatingly cool voice or that ability to make her feel ridiculous with the mere lift of an eyebrow. Polly was abruptly conscious of how she must look with her frilly cap and apron and her wildly unsuitable shoes.

'What on earth are *you* doing here?' she demanded, ruffled in spite of herself.

'Looking for you.'

'For me? What's the matter?' What if Simon had come to break some bad news to her? Quick concern deepened the blue in Polly's eyes as instant scenarios of disaster chased each other across her mind. 'Are Mum and Dad all right?' she asked anxiously.

'They're fine,' said Simon, and she blew out a breath of relief. 'They've just been wondering the same about you. I had lunch with them last week, and they were worried because they hadn't heard from you for a while. Apparently all they've had is a couple of very uninformative postcards since you arrived so I said that I would stop by and check that you were all right on my way to La Treille.'

'Oh, dear.' Polly grimaced ruefully. 'I should have given them a ring. I meant to, but I knew they'd ask what the job was like and I've never been any good at lying, so I'd have had to tell them how crummy it was.

I made such a big thing about what a fantastic job it was going to be that I didn't want to admit that I'd ended up as a glorified maid!'

'How did you get to be a maid? I thought you were going to be assistant to a film director?'

'That's what *I* thought, too,' said Polly bitterly. She glanced over her shoulder to make sure that Martine Sterne hadn't come out to greet the latest arrival. She would have a fit if she caught Polly having a private conversation in the middle of the party. 'I thought I'd be swanking around the Cannes Film Festival with a clipboard and fending off the stars, but it turns out that Rushford Sterne's last movie was a flop so he's the one trying to get to the stars for support, not the other way round. He's trying to raise money for a new project, so they've been doing lots of entertaining, and all they want me for is to open doors and serve drinks and wash up and generally be a sort of household slave!'

Simon looked disapproving. Not that there was anything new in that, Polly thought, resigned. He had disapproved of her as long as he had known her, which was her entire life.

Their parents were good friends, and the two families had gone on holidays together every year when they were children. When she was a tiny girl, Polly had adored Simon, who was seven years older, and she had been teased ever since about the way she had followed him around everywhere and asked him to marry her when she was four. It hadn't taken her long to grow out of *that*, though. Nearer in age to his brother and sister, Polly had allied herself with Charlie and Emily, who were much more fun, and Simon had become the boring, sensible older brother who had tried to keep them all under control.

'Why do you stay if the job's so awful?' he asked her now.

'It's a matter of principle,' said Polly grandly.

Simon's brow lifted. 'Principle?'

'Well, maybe not principle,' she admitted, 'but Dad advised me so strongly against taking the job that I can't go back now and admit that he was right. He said it all sounded too vague and that if I wasn't careful I'd end up being exploited, which is exactly what has happened,' she added glumly. 'I was so determined to prove to him that he was wrong that I refused to take any of the money he offered me, and now I couldn't afford to go even if I wanted to. I had to pay my own fare here, and I haven't been paid yet, so I've got about five pounds to see me through to the end of my contract at the moment!'

'No wonder your parents worry about you!' said Simon with a shake of his head.

'It's not that bad,' said Polly defensively. 'At least I'm seeing how the other half live! This is a fabulous house, and I get to meet loads of glamorous people, even if it is only to offer them a drink.'

Simon was predictably unimpressed. 'I don't see much advantage in a job where the most exciting thing you do is hand out drinks to a lot of rich, overdressed people who could perfectly well get their own!'

'No, well, you wouldn't,' she said crossly.

That was typical of Simon, of course! Frivolity was completely alien to him. It was a shame, really. When he let down his guard and relaxed, he could be good fun, but most of the time he was infuriatingly superior and sensible.

Look at him! He must be the only person in the South of France wearing a suit and tie, Polly thought with a mental roll of her eyes. It might be a lightweight suit, and the tie might be a—for him—daring shade of yellow, but it was still a suit and tie. Why didn't he wear a bowler hat, carry a rolled-up umbrella and be done with it?

She glanced over her shoulder again as the sounds of the party rang down the hall, suddenly loud as if someone had opened a door. 'Look, I have to get back, Simon,' she said. 'Mrs Sterne will be furious if she finds me out here talking to you. I'm sorry you've come out of your way to see me, but really, I'm fine. I'll ring Mum and Dad tomorrow and tell them to stop flapping.'

Completely ignoring her attempts to close the door, Simon stepped coolly past her into the hall. 'Can't I come in for a minute?' he asked. 'I picked up the car at the airport and came straight here, so I could do with a break from travelling.'

'No!' said Polly, with another harried glance over her shoulder. Martine Sterne would be on the rampage any minute, wanting to know who was at the door, accusing her of slacking, ordering her back to work with her snapping fingers.

'I mean, I'd love to invite you in,' she said hurriedly as Simon looked at her in surprise, 'but I just haven't got time tonight. The Sternes are having a party, as you can probably hear, and I've got to work.'

'Don't mind me,' said Simon casually. 'I'll just join the party. I'll take a look at all these glamorous and exciting people you're so thrilled to meet.'

Under Polly's horrified gaze, he strolled off in the direction of the noise. For a moment she was too appalled to move, then she leapt after him and grabbed his arm. 'What are you *doing*?' she demanded in an anguished undertone, coming as close as she could to shouting in a whisper. 'You can't go in there!'

'Why not?'

He was winding her up, Polly realised furiously. Simon had always had a disconcerting ability to keep a perfectly straight face, but she recognised that gleam of mockery in his pale grey eyes. 'You're not invited,' she pointed out through gritted teeth.

'I don't suppose anyone will mind,' he said and cocked his head as if listening. 'They all sound as if they're well away in there,' he went on, moving inexorably towards the party as if oblivious to Polly hanging grimly onto him. 'Nobody's going to notice one more, are they?'

'Simon, please, stop messing around!' Polly leant back and tried to dig her heels into the smooth marble floor to slow him down. She hadn't realised Simon was quite that strong. It was like trying to manoeuvre a rock.

To her intense relief, he hesitated just before the door, and, seizing her opportunity, Polly swung him round and began pushing him back towards the front door. 'I don't know what you think you're playing at, but it isn't funny!' she said crossly. 'Martine will kill me if she finds you here!'

Bundling him before her, she managed to get Simon as far as the door, only to commit a tactical error by letting go of his arm so that she could pull the door open wide and shove him through it. Immediately, Simon headed back to the party.

'I can't believe your employers would mind you inviting a friend to their party,' he said provocatively. 'It's not as if I'll embarrass you.'

'You don't know my employers,' panted Polly as she

grabbed his arm once more and dragged him forcibly back to the door. 'And, as far as I'm concerned, you're not a friend any more! Now, will you please just *go*?'

'Polly!' Polly's worst fears were realised as Martine Sterne's shocked voice rang out behind her, and she spun round, still clutching Simon's arm.

'Now look what you've done!' she muttered as her employer advanced furiously down the hall towards them. 'If you don't want me to tell my father that you've ruined my job, you'd better pretend to be a total stranger!' she added out of the side of her mouth in a savage undertone. 'I might get away with it if she thinks I'm just trying to get rid of a gatecrasher. If you let on that I've ever laid eyes on you before, I'll never forgive you!'

'What are you doing, Polly?' Martine demanded in a voice like a whiplash, and then, as Polly opened her mouth to launch into her gatecrasher story, added, 'Let go of M. Taverner *at once*!'

Polly's jaw dropped.

'You'll catch flies like that if you're not careful,' murmured Simon. Removing his arm from Polly's suddenly nerveless grasp, he made a great show of straightening his jacket and shooting his cuffs as if emerging from a frantic tussle.

Before Polly had a chance to grasp what was going on, Martine was holding out her hands to Simon with a smile that Polly hadn't known that she possessed. 'It is such a pleasure to see you, M. Taverner, again—or may I call you Simon?' she said in her charmingly accented English.

Polly boggled as Simon took both Martine's hands and kissed her cheeks in the French fashion. 'I was beginning to wonder if I had the right house,' he said with a maliciously amused glance at Polly who was watching them with a dumbfounded expression, her mouth opening and closing like a landed fish. 'Your maid seemed rather reluctant to admit me.'

'*Maid?*' Polly was outraged, but was silenced by a venomous glance from Martine.

'Be quiet!' she snapped. 'I'm so sorry, Simon,' she went on in a caressing voice at variance with the furious expression in her eyes when she looked at Polly. 'She is quite new and doesn't know what she is doing.'

'But—' Polly opened her mouth to object.

'I said, *be quiet*!' flashed Martine. Turning back to Simon, she forced a smile. 'You must forgive her. Now, let's go and find Rushford. I know he's looking forward to meeting you again.'

Polly shook her head experimentally. It didn't *feel* like a nightmare, but perhaps it was. How else could Simon Taverner be here, apparently on the best of terms with her employer? There was something horribly real about him, though. He looked so familiar. How many times in the past had she seen that look of unholy amusement in his eyes as he had got the better of her? Look at him now, taking off his jacket, holding it out to her! He *was* real…and that meant this was really happening!

'Perhaps your maid could take my jacket for me?' he said to Martine, who jerked her head at Polly.

'I expect she could manage that,' she said, not even bothering to disguise her sarcasm, and Polly somehow found herself holding out her hand and taking the jacket.

'I—I think there's been some mistake,' she stammered.

'There has indeed,' said Martine with a glacial look,

'but we will discuss it tomorrow, not now. You've wasted enough of M. Taverner's time already!'

'But—'

'You're supposed to be serving drinks,' Martine interrupted her in a voice that could have sliced through steel. 'I suggest that you get back to it if you want to keep your job until tomorrow.'

And with that she bore Simon off into the party, leaving Polly open-mouthed in the middle of the hall, Simon's jacket hanging from her hand. Simon had even had the effrontery to wink at her as they'd left!

Head reeling, Polly stood there and stared after them with a bemused expression, still not quite convinced that she hadn't dreamed it all.

Perhaps she had slipped into another reality, and there was another Simon Taverner, a different Simon who might conceivably have some connection with the Sternes? But surely no other Simon could look like that, so ordinary and yet so utterly, infuriatingly self-assured at the same time? No one else could have that deadpan expression or those acute grey eyes with their glint of mockery.

Lifting Simon's jacket to her face, Polly sniffed at it. It even *smelt* like Simon, she thought, and was taken aback at how vividly the faint, cleanly masculine scent of his clothes brought him to mind. She hadn't known that his smell was so familiar to her. It seemed such an oddly intimate thing to recognise about Simon that she jerked her head back as if she had been caught prying. She didn't like to imagine what Emily or Charlie would have said if they had seen her burying her face in Simon's jacket like a lovestruck teenager!

Embarrassed at herself, Polly hung the jacket firmly up in the cloakroom and picked up the tray of drinks.

Simon had some explaining to do when she caught up with him!

Sidling back into the party, she scanned the crowd in search of him, still not entirely sure that the whole thing hadn't been a bad dream brought on by too much hard work. But no! There he was, flanked by the fawning Sternes who were obsequiously introducing him to a whole group of celebrities!

Polly's heart did an odd little somersault as she spotted him. It was all very odd. This was Simon, the boy who had directed all the games on holiday, who had teased her and later ignored her, who was the closest thing she had to an older, exasperating brother. True, it was years since they had spent any time together, but he had seemed just the same when she had seen him at Emily's wedding last year, and he couldn't have changed that much since then...could he?

Absently, Polly offered drinks, hardly noticing whether anyone accepted or not. Why were they all making such a fuss of him? It wasn't because of his looks or style, that was for sure. As far as fashion went, he was a non-starter in that shirt and tie, and the room was chock-a-block with actors who were far more handsome than Simon could ever hope to be.

Not that Simon was bad-looking, she admitted to herself, eyeing him judiciously, but there was nothing special about him either. He had brown hair, grey eyes, a quiet, unremarkable face. He was just ordinary. He was just Simon.

So why did he make everyone else look overdressed and vaguely out of place?

Polly watched him, a puzzled frown between her brows. She couldn't get over the way Simon seemed to be the focus of the party. Perhaps it was his air of stillness and detachment that made him stand out in the crowd? It wasn't as if he were doing anything to draw attention to himself. Quite the contrary. He was just standing there, looking faintly bored, while around him people whom Polly would have given her eye-teeth to meet were making extravagant gestures and exclamations in an effort to gain his interest.

The tray forgotten in her hands, Polly stood among the chattering crowd and looked at Simon as if she had never seen him before. It was oddly unsettling to realise that, where she had always dismissed him as boring and stuffy, others might see restraint and quiet authority.

Not only that, some of them clearly found that indefinable aura of power very attractive. Polly's blue eyes narrowed as she saw a beautiful actress laugh and run her fingers suggestively down his arm. She didn't know what was more irritating—the way the actress was pawing him or the way Simon was simply ignoring her.

It was at that moment that Simon chose to look round and encountered Polly's baleful blue gaze. She scowled at him across the room, but, instead of looking suitably penitent for the way he had jeopardised her job, Simon only smiled, a swift, wicked smile that transformed his quiet face, and Polly was furious to find herself abruptly breathless.

As everyone around him turned jealously to see who had succeeded in attracting his interest, Polly put up her chin and jerked round, presenting him with a view of her rigid back. She was mortified at being caught staring at him, and it didn't help to realise just how much he was enjoying the situation. Not only had he let her make a complete fool of herself in front of

Martine, but now he had to rub it in by showing off to all his admirers while she was left to hand around drinks! Polly could just hear him telling her father about this evening, and how the fantastic job she had boasted about had turned out to be nothing more than a lowly waitress!

'You seem to be very interested in Simon Taverner.'

Polly jumped as Philippe appeared beside her. As he took a glass from her tray and raised it to her in a silent toast she was conscious of an obscure sense of resentment. Six weeks she had spent dreaming of the moment when Philippe would seek her out, and now thanks to Simon she had been too cross to appreciate it!

'Simon Taverner?' she echoed cautiously. How on earth did *Philippe* know Simon?

'The man you've been watching for the last half-hour,' said Philippe with one of his smiles. 'Just like I've been watching *you*,' he added almost casually, and a little thrill went through Polly.

Philippe had been watching her! Maybe the shoes had done the trick after all! Polly's sore feet were forgotten as she realised that after all these weeks Philippe was actually standing there, talking to her. Dazzled by his good looks—he was even more handsome close up!—Polly sought desperately for a way to prolong the conversation. She had to make sure he didn't think she was interested in Simon, for a start!

'Simon Taverner?' she said as carelessly as she could. 'That dull-looking man talking to your sister? Is that his name?'

Philippe looked amused. 'He is far from dull. Simon Taverner owns a major investment company.'

'That sounds pretty dull to me,' said Polly. She had known Simon was something to do with finance but she had never taken much interest in it. Her father was always raving about how successful Simon was, but investment didn't seem much fun to Polly. It sounded like the kind of typically safe, boring career Simon *would* choose.

'It's not dull when you make as much money as Simon Taverner does,' said Philippe dryly.

Polly stared at him. 'You mean he's *rich*?'

Philippe laughed at her astonishment. 'He has a very understated style, doesn't he? You might not think it to look at him, but Simon Taverner could buy out half the people in this room. He's a big player.'

'Really?' Polly wondered if Philippe was joking. Simon came from a comfortable background, and she had heard enough from her father to know that he had done well, but *rich*?

'Why do you think my sister invited him tonight? She's hoping that he'll put some money into Rushford's new project.'

'You mean he invests in *movies*?' Polly goggled at him. She didn't think she could take any more surprises tonight. She had never known Simon watch a video, let alone go out to a movie.

'It's people like Simon Taverner who run the entertainment industry,' Philippe told her. 'Their names never appear in the credits, but they're the ones who can make or break a film. Taverner's interest may be financial, but he knows what he's doing all right. If he invests in your film, you're onto a box-office success.'

'*Really?*' It was all too much to take in. Unthinkingly, Polly turned to look back at Simon. He was looking towards her, almost as if he knew that they were talking about him, and as their eyes met across the room Polly was conscious of a peculiar charge twanging through her like an electric shock.

Oddly jolted, she jerked her eyes away to find Philippe watching her with a speculative expression. 'It looks as if M. Taverner is interested in you, too!'

'I'm not interested in him.' Polly tried to laugh. 'And if he's as rich and successful as you say, he's not likely to be interested in me either, is he?'

'Oh, I don't know,' said Philippe, lazily appraising her. 'You're a pretty girl, Polly. Very pretty, in fact.'

Polly glowed. She loved the way Philippe said her name. Pol*lee*. It sounded so much better in a French accent.

'Really?' she said breathlessly. It was all she seemed to be able to say to him this evening. She had to extend her vocabulary or he would think her English was as bad as her French.

'Really.' Philippe smiled. He had very white, even teeth and his eyes crinkled irresistibly. 'Did you think I hadn't noticed?'

Flustered, Polly wondered what she was supposed to say to that, but fortunately he didn't seem to expect a reply. 'I never seem to get a chance to talk to you,' he went on. 'Martine keeps you very busy, doesn't she?'

She certainly did, thought Polly with feeling. She'd better not say that, though. After all, Martine *was* his sister. Much better to sound enthusiastic. 'I like having lots to do,' she lied instead.

'So how long are you going to be working for Rushford?'

'Until they go back to the States.'

'You're not going with them?'

Polly shook her head. 'I want to stay in France,' she said, omitting to mention that the chances of Martine asking her to go anywhere with them were non-existent. It wasn't that Polly hadn't done her best, but Martine had taken against her from the start, and was constantly criticising. 'I want to improve my French,' she told Philippe, 'but your sister and Rushford speak English, and so do all their visitors, so I've hardly spoken it since I arrived.'

'Well, if you want to speak French you must certainly stay in France. Are you going to look for another job, or just travel around?'

'A bit of both, I expect.'

'If you're travelling towards Marsillac, you must come and see me,' said Philippe with another charming smile.

Polly was thrilled. 'Could I really?'

'Of course.' Philippe pulled a card out of his breast pocket and slid it under Polly's thumb where it was holding the tray. 'Here's my address.'

'Th-thank you,' stuttered Polly, hardly able to believe her luck. She wanted to hug herself. A smile from Philippe was enough to have her walking on air, but now she had not only talked to him, but he had told her that she was pretty *and* he had invited her to visit him! The evening which had taken such a disastrous turn with Simon's arrival was suddenly sparkling and golden with promise.

With a last dreamy look after Philippe, Polly turned with her tray only to bump into Simon, who had come up behind her and was wearing an expression that was even more severe than usual.

'Who was that?' he demanded.

'Philippe Ladurie,' sighed Polly, too happy to resent his tone. 'Isn't he gorgeous?'

Simon snorted as he looked over at Philippe, who

had been captured by a beautiful redhead. 'So that's Philippe Ladurie! I've heard about him. One of these playboys that run around living above their means with no talent for anything except getting invited to parties and breaking up marriages!'

'He's very nice,' said Polly defiantly. She wasn't going to let Simon spoil her wonderful evening. Philippe had said she was pretty and he had invited her to stay. What did it matter what Simon thought?

'You would think so,' said Simon. 'You always did have lousy taste in men!'

In spite of her resolve to ignore him, Polly flushed indignantly. 'I do not!'

'Only you could be impressed by a man like that,' Simon went on inexorably. 'Look at him, he's so smarmy and self-satisfied I'm surprised he doesn't slip on all that smug charm he's oozing!'

'At least he has charm!' she retorted. 'You wouldn't recognise charm if it jumped up and punched you on the nose!'

'Martine Sterne thinks I'm charming,' Simon pointed out provocatively.

Polly glared at him, reminded of that scene in the hall. 'Do you want to tell me exactly what you're doing here, Simon?'

'I told you, I came to check that you were all right.'

'Oh, yes, and you just happened to have an invitation to Martine Sterne's party in your pocket?'

His mouth twitched at her sarcasm. 'Not exactly. Martine Sterne is always sending me invitations, which I always chuck away. She just assumed that I'd re-membered there was a party tonight—' He broke off as he saw Polly shift from one foot to the other and wince. 'What *are* you doing?'

'My feet hurt.' Polly felt like telling Simon that it was his fault. She hadn't even noticed how agonising her shoes were when she'd been talking to Philippe.

'Well, we'll sit down, then,' said Simon briskly, looking around for some seats, but she shook her head so vigorously that her cap slipped askew again.

'I can't do that! Martine would sack me on the spot if she saw me sitting down!'

He sighed. 'All right, we'll go outside.'

'I don't know...' Polly hesitated, and Simon frowned as he looked at her more closely.

'Come on, just for five minutes. You look as if you could do with taking the weight off your feet.'

The thought was irresistible. Polly looked longingly at the door leading out onto the terrace. 'There's a table down by the pool,' she said. 'No one would see us down there, would they?'

Simon sighed. 'Martine Sterne's not really that bad, is she?'

'She is!' Polly looked around her nervously, but Martine was busy talking to a famous actor who Polly had been disappointed to see was much smaller than he appeared on screen. 'You have to promise me that if anyone notices us you'll say that it was all your idea!'

'They won't notice,' said Simon acidly. 'They're all so busy congratulating themselves on being beautiful that they wouldn't notice if we stripped off and did the cancan. If you're going to come, let's go!'

CHAPTER TWO

'THAT'S better!' Polly dumped the tray on the table and sank gratefully down onto a chair. To Simon's exasperation, she had insisted on an elaborate and, in his opinion, quite unnecessary subterfuge, sending him out through the terrace door while she slipped out a separate exit a few minutes later.

He watched her ease off her shoes with much wincing and grimacing and swing up her legs to rest them on the table. 'Why do you always have to make life so difficult for yourself, Polly?' he asked austerely. 'Anyone else who knew they were going to be serving drinks all evening would have put on a pair of sensible shoes, not those ridiculous things!'

'I know, but I thought they might detract from this stupid uniform,' she explained, pulling off her cap and fanning herself with it. 'I look dowdy enough without sensible shoes as well!'

Simon looked at her. Her hair, rather blonder than he remembered, had been piled haphazardly on top of her head, but most of it had slipped down in wispy strands around her hot face. There was always something vaguely dishevelled about Polly, he thought, no matter how much effort she put into her appearance. She even made the prim white blouse that Martine Sterne had no doubt chosen look somehow rumpled and sexy—

Sexy? Simon's thoughts broke off abruptly. Where had that word come from? He couldn't think of *Polly*

as sexy! He shook himself mentally. Surely the word
he had been looking for was... He searched his mind
with growing unease for a substitute. Messy! Yes, that
was it, he decided with some relief. He rewound mentally.

She even made the prim white blouse look somehow
rumpled and *messy*.

Much better.

Wrenching his eyes away from the shadowy cleavage he could just glimpse between the open buttons,
Simon let his gaze travel on down to the frilly apron
and on to the long, bare brown legs resting on the table.
He had never really noticed what spectacular legs she
had before.

'I can think of many words to describe you, Polly,'
he said dryly, 'but dowdy isn't one of them!'

There was an odd note in his voice. Polly was suddenly very conscious of his eyes on her legs and
brought them abruptly to the ground. 'Never mind my
shoes, anyway!' she said sharply to disguise the strange
tingle under her skin where his gaze had rested. 'I want
to know why you didn't tell me you knew the Sternes,
and—more to the point—why you didn't tell Martine
you knew *me*!'

'You told me not to,' Simon pointed out, all injured
innocence, and she scowled at him.

'You know perfectly well that was only because I
thought she'd be livid to find you in the house! You
could have told me that Martine would fall on your
neck when she saw you!'

'You were so busy trying to hustle me out of the
door, I didn't get a chance to tell you anything!'

'Oh, *sure*!' There had been moments tonight, like
just now when he had looked at her legs, when Polly

had been uncomfortably aware of Simon as a man, and it was almost a relief to discover that he was still the same supremely irritating friend of the family. 'As if anyone had ever been able to stop you saying what you wanted!' she accused him. 'You just thought it would be much more fun to let me make a complete idiot of myself!'

Simon held up his hands in mock surrender. 'All right, I admit it! I couldn't resist teasing you, but, if it's any comfort, I got my comeuppance. I had no intention of going to the party, but once Martine had seen me I didn't have much choice. I've only just managed to escape from Rushford Sterne's clutches!' He looked sideways at Polly, and his mouth quirked. 'It was worth it to see your face when Martine greeted me, though!'

'I'm glad I've provided you with so much amusement,' said Polly sourly. 'I suppose it never occurred to you that I might lose my job over that?'

'I didn't realise that Martine was quite such a difficult woman to deal with, I must say. I'm sorry. I'll talk to her, if you like, and explain that it was all my fault.'

'Then she'll feel a fool and she'll be even worse,' Polly objected. She sat up straighter in her chair. 'Perhaps you could offer to invest in Rushford's new movie and then she'll be in such a good mood she'll forget about me,' she suggested hopefully.

'I'm not that sorry!' said Simon with an astringent look. 'I'd rather get you a new job! Rushford's just been telling me at length about this project, and as far as I can see it's got disaster written all over it.'

Polly folded her arms and rested them on the table. 'Do you really invest in movies?' It was still hard to believe.

'I invest in all sorts of things. The entertainment industry is big business nowadays, but it's just one sector of our investments.'

In spite of herself, Polly was impressed. 'I couldn't believe it when Philippe told me,' she confessed. 'I had no idea you were rich!'

'If I'd known you were so interested in my bank balance, I'd have sent you copies of my statements.'

His sarcasm went over Polly's head. She was still trying to assimilate this new side to Simon. 'I can't understand why nobody told me,' she said almost to herself. 'I mean, I knew you had a house in Provence, and Dad's always going on about how successful you are, but I didn't realise that you were *that* rich! Does Emily know?'

Simon's mouth twitched. She made it sound as if his money were a guilty secret. 'I expect that she knows that I have my own company, but no doubt, like you, she has absolutely no idea of what I actually do. It's not a secret. If either of you had ever shown any interest in me, you would have known just like everyone else.'

Polly blew out her breath as she sat back. 'Well, I would never have believed it!'

'Why on earth not?'

'It just seems all wrong,' she tried to explain. 'I've always thought of you as old Simon, pootling into the office every day to do something boring with money, and suddenly I find you're some kind of jet-setting tycoon! The way Philippe was carrying on, you probably get invited to parties like this all the time!'

'I get invited, but I rarely go,' snapped Simon, nettled to discover just how boring Polly thought he was.

'See! That's exactly what I mean about it feeling wrong!' Polly rubbed her sore toes. 'Money's wasted on you, Simon. You've got no appreciation of glamour or excitement. Now, if it was me, it would be different,' she said, considering the matter judiciously. 'I'd love a jet-set lifestyle. That's what I thought I'd be getting when I took this job. The closest I ever seem to get is handing out champagne for other people to drink,' she added, gloomily remembering her menial position.

'I don't know why you don't get yourself a proper job,' said Simon irritably.

'Don't start! You sound just like Dad!'

'It's not as if you're not capable,' he went on, ignoring her. 'You can be quite intelligent when you try. You're wasted on all these temporary jobs you do. You never seem to stay anywhere longer than a couple of months.'

'Yes, I do,' said Polly, affronted. 'I spent six months working in that ski resort, and I was on the cruise ship even longer than that!'

'It's hardly an impressive track record, is it? I thought it was men who were supposed to have a fear of commitment?'

'I'm not afraid of commitment,' she said with dignity. 'I'm just not prepared to commit myself to anything—a job, a relationship, *anything*—unless I'm going to see it through. That's something different from being afraid. I don't see any point in launching into a career unless I'm sure that it's what I really want to do.'

Simon was patently unconvinced. 'When are you going to decide what it is that you want?' he asked sardonically.

'I don't know,' said Polly, 'but I expect I'll recognise it when it comes along. And in the meantime I'd rather try lots of different things and have a good time

while I'm at it. I know it drives Dad mad, but I don't
think I'm being irresponsible.' She tilted her chin
proudly. 'My contracts may not be for very long, but
I always fulfil them.'

'How long is this contract?'

'Three months.' She sighed. 'Still over six weeks to
go. I can't say I'll be sorry to get to the end of this
one. It has to be the worst job I've ever done. It's not
even as if I'm getting a decent wage either. The honour
of being bossed around by Martine Sterne all summer
is supposed to be enough, I think. Oh, well.'

Leaning down, she forced her poor feet back into
her shoes and stood up gingerly. 'I'd better get back
before Martine sees me. She'd be furious if she knew
that a lowly wage-slave like me was out here with her
guest of honour. It spoils the tone of her party!'

'I'd rather talk to you than any of that lot in there,'
said Simon, getting to his feet as well.

Polly grinned. 'Why, Simon! I think that's the nicest
thing you've ever said to me!'

'It's not saying much,' he pointed out. 'Are you sure
you're all right here, Polly? If you need money in case
anything goes wrong…'

'Nothing's going to go wrong,' she said firmly, waving his offer aside. 'Thanks anyway, but I'm absolutely
fine.' Grimacing as her shoes pinched at her feet, she
picked up the tray. 'Are you going back to the party?'

'Not likely! I'm off,' said Simon. 'What did you do
with my jacket?'

'In the cloakroom,' said Polly. 'And think yourself
lucky it's not screwed in a heap on the floor after that
maid crack!'

Simon only gave one of his swift, disconcerting

smiles. 'Goodbye, Polly,' he said, and then to Polly's surprise he flicked her cheek with his finger. 'Be good!'

Polly stared after him as he strolled back towards the terrace, absurdly aware of her face burning where his finger had grazed her skin. She felt rather peculiar. It was just Simon, walking out of her life again as casually as he had walked back into it. That was all their relationship was now, a brief meeting every year or so, characterised by a mixture of snappiness and teasing and comforting familiarity. So why did she suddenly feel as if she wanted to call him back?

Polly shook her head. Why was she standing here thinking about Simon? Philippe was inside, and she would much rather be thinking about him! Serving drinks might not be much fun, but at least she would get the chance to see him, even if she was only able to gaze wistfully at him from a distance.

'What do you think you've been doing?' Martine Sterne's voice made Polly jump as she stepped through the doors, and the tray tilted dangerously in her hands.

'M-Mrs Sterne!' she stuttered, just managing to rescue the sliding glasses in time. 'I…er, I just wondered if there was anyone outside who would like a drink.'

'Don't lie!' Martine's voice was like a whiplash. 'You were out there with Simon Taverner! I saw you follow him out, so you needn't try and deny it.'

'It's not what you think,' said Polly, eyeing her employer nervously. Martine's face was white with rage. Perhaps she should tell her the truth? 'Simon actually came to see me.'

'To see you?' Martine gave a contemptuous laugh. 'Simon Taverner isn't likely to be interested in anyone like you, is he?'

'But he is! He's a friend of mine.'

'A friend who doesn't know your name? A friend you didn't even want to let in the house?'

Polly gritted her teeth. It would be hopeless trying to explain her relationship with Simon to Martine in this mood. She wasn't likely to be impressed by him being a friend of the family either. But what if she pretended to Martine that Simon was closer than he really was? Polly seized on the idea. Surely if Martine thought that she was special to her precious Simon she would calm down and change her tune? She might even be nice to her!

'He's more than a friend. He's my...my fiancé,' she said with an edge of desperation.

'Oh, yes?' sneered Martine. 'And why would Simon Taverner's fiancée be reduced to doing a job like yours?'

Polly swallowed. 'We...we had a terrible row,' she improvised wildly. 'I decided I had to get away for a while, so I applied for this job and then Simon found out where I was and followed me down here.' It sounded a bit thin, but it was the best she could do on the spur of the moment. 'I didn't want to talk to him at first,' she went on, gaining confidence, 'and when you saw us in the hall, I was trying to get him to leave because I didn't realise that he knew you.' That last bit was true, anyway! 'Then he persuaded me to meet him outside, and we've sorted everything out.'

'So now you're engaged again?' Martine's voice dripped with disbelief.

'Yes.'

'And he's gone off and left you again?'

'Yes.' She didn't even sound convinced by her own story, Polly thought wryly. 'Simon knows I want to carry on working for you until the end of my contract,' she added, not that anyone in their right mind would believe *that* either!

Martine certainly didn't. 'Stop lying, you stupid girl!' she snapped.

There was a spark of anger in Polly's eyes. She was blessed with a normally sunny nature, but she had a temper too, and at that moment she was having a hard time holding onto it!

'Why don't you ask Simon Taverner if I'm lying or not?'

Martine took up the challenge. 'Yes, why don't I do that?' she answered grimly.

Simon had his hand on the front door when he heard Martine Sterne's voice calling his name. Sighing inwardly, he turned with an excuse for leaving early on his lips, only to see her stalking towards him with Polly hobbling defiantly in her wake.

'Perhaps you can clear up a little misunderstanding, Simon,' said Martine, forcing a smile to her lips although her eyes were still glittering with rage. 'Polly here tells me that you are engaged!'

'It's true, isn't it, darling?' Polly nipped in front of Martine and slipped her hand into his with a warning pinch. 'You came all the way down here to ask me to marry you!'

She smiled confidently up at him, sure that he wouldn't let her down. Simon might be immensely irritating at times, but you could always rely on him. On countless occasions when they were children, he had helped Emily, Charlie and her out of scrapes, and although they had giggled and rolled their eyes when he had ticked them off, not once had he told their parents what they had been doing, when they would have got into real trouble.

'I know we agreed to keep it a secret, but you don't mind Mrs Sterne knowing, do you?'

Simon looked down into Polly's pleading blue eyes and sighed inwardly again. He didn't know what she was up to, but it didn't look as if he had much choice other than to play along.

'Of course not,' he agreed woodenly, and was rewarded with a dazzling smile as Polly gave his hand a grateful squeeze.

'I don't believe you!' Martine said in a voice shaking with fury. 'She's got some kind of hold over you! She's making you do this!'

'Why would she want to do that?' asked Simon politely.

'And as for you!' Martine rounded on Polly. 'How dare you come here under false pretences?'

'But I didn't—'

'You lied to me deliberately!'

'I just want to finish my contract,' said Polly helplessly. She had hoped that Simon's influence would save her job, but it looked as if his support had simply enraged Martine further. 'Simon's going, but I'll stay.'

'Stay?' Martine echoed malevolently. 'I'm not having you in my house a moment longer and you needn't think you're going to get any money either! You've been a disaster ever since you arrived. You're the worst girl we've ever had working for us—messy and inefficient and insolent and lazy!'

'*Lazy?*'

Simon felt Polly stiffen in outrage. 'I think you've said quite enough, Mrs Sterne,' he said coldly. He put his arm around Polly's shoulders. 'I wouldn't let Polly stay here now if you went down and kissed her feet! Go and get your things, Polly,' he went on. 'I'm taking you away from here.' He turned back to Martine who was glaring in impotent fury. 'After the way you've treated Polly, you can tell your husband not to bother contacting me again. I won't be investing in any of his films!'

'Now what?'

Polly looked at Simon as he tossed the last of her assorted carrier bags into the back of his car and closed the door. A mixture of adrenaline, rage and euphoria at the expression on Martine's face had carried her up to her room to collect her things together, but at Simon's question it began to dawn on her that she had no money, no job and nowhere to go.

'I don't know,' she admitted.

Simon watched her push her hair wearily behind her ears, and something shifted inside him. 'Well, you can't stay here,' he said gruffly, opening the passenger door for her. 'You'd better get in.'

Polly slumped into the front seat and pulled off her shoes. 'What a disaster!' she sighed as Simon pushed the key into the ignition.

'So much for you fulfilling every contract,' he said dryly. 'What on earth possessed you to tell Martine Sterne we were engaged?'

'It seemed like a good idea at the time,' said Polly. 'Martine seemed so keen on you that I thought she might be a bit nicer to me if I was your fiancée. Thanks for backing me up, by the way. She would never have believed me if it hadn't been for you.'

'It didn't seem to have quite the effect you wanted, though, did it?'

'I was obviously going to get sacked anyway,' she pointed out. 'And at least this way I got to see her face when you told her you wouldn't let me stay if she went down on her knees and kissed my feet!' Polly perked up at the memory. Martine's chagrined expression as she had realised just how badly she had miscalculated almost made losing her job worthwhile!

'Let's just hope she feels humiliated enough to keep that little scene to herself,' said Simon. 'What else did you tell her?'

'Nothing really. I just said that we were engaged, that we'd had a row and that you'd followed me down here because you couldn't bear to live without me a second longer.'

'Good God!' he said, revolted. 'No wonder she didn't believe you!'

Polly bridled. 'It's not that far-fetched!'

'It is if you know anything about me, or anything about you!'

'Well, none of those people there tonight do, so it won't matter even if Martine does tell them. You said yourself that you don't often go to parties like that, so they won't know you—and they certainly don't know me!'

'Maybe not, but it wouldn't stop them gossiping anyway. You must know what those people are like. Gossip is all they have to do, and a story like that would get back to London in five minutes, where people *do* know me. I don't want to go home and find that everyone thinks I've been running around France supposedly making an idiot of myself over you!'

'I hadn't thought of that,' said Polly in a remorseful voice. 'It could be quite embarrassing, couldn't it? You'd better ring Helena and tell her that it was all my fault in case she hears anything.' She frowned as a thought struck her. 'Where is Helena, anyway?'

There was a tiny pause. 'She's working,' said Simon curtly.

She looked at him in surprise. 'Are you here on business, then? I thought you said you were going to your house in Provence...what's it called again?'

'La Treille.'

'Yes, that's it. Lovely name.' Polly had heard lots about the old farmhouse that Simon had restored. She had never been there herself, but her parents and Emily had, and all had waxed lyrical about how beautiful it was. 'Are you going on your own, then?'

'I'm meeting friends there,' he said uninformatively.

Polly wondered why he was being so cagey. 'Didn't Helena want to come?' she asked nosily, and Simon's mouth turned down at the corners. He didn't want to talk about Helena.

'She was going to come, but unfortunately an important job came up at the last minute and she had to stay in London.' It wasn't the whole truth, but it was good enough for Polly. She had never liked Helena, and he wasn't in the mood to hear her enthusing over the end of his relationship with her.

The car was warm and luxurious. Polly settled herself more comfortably into her seat and yawned as tiredness caught up with her. 'I can't imagine giving up a holiday to work.'

'Not everyone has your relaxed attitude to a career,' said Simon with something of a snap. 'Helena is a professional. She can't just walk out because she feels like it.'

'But...don't you mind?'

'No,' he said somewhat defensively. 'I've always understood how important her career is to her. It's one of the things I respect most about her. She's a very

talented lawyer.' All of that was true. What had thrown
him was discovering that the talented lawyer had suddenly decided that the career she had talked so much
about suddenly wasn't enough.

Polly sighed to herself, remembering how Simon had
brought Helena to Emily's wedding. She and Emily
had been amazed that he should turn up with someone
so glamorous. Perhaps if they'd known how successful
Simon was they might not have been so surprised.
Helena was beautiful and clever and stylish, and she
made Polly feel like a galumphing adolescent. It had
been a relief to discover that the rest of the family,
including Simon's mother, found Helena as intimidat-
ing as she did.

She studied Simon from under her lashes. In the
darkness, his face was lit from below by the lights on
the dashboard. Their dim glow emphasised the line of
his nose and jaw, glancing off the stern mouth and
blurring the lean angles of his cheek, and something
stirred queerly inside her as she looked at him.

He was so familiar and yet suddenly a stranger, and
for the first time Polly understood what a girl like
Helena saw in him. They were well matched, both
clever, both independent, both successful.

For some reason, Polly sighed again. She didn't want
to hear about Helena's wonderful career when her own
was in disarray yet again. She had been so determined
to make a success of her job with the Sternes too!
Helena would never be reduced to making up silly stories. *She* would never have been sacked. She would
never have been doing a job like that in the first place.

On the other hand, Helena had to work when she
could be on holiday. Ever buoyant, Polly told herself
to look on the bright side. Helena hadn't met Philippe,

had she? Maybe being sacked would turn out to be the best thing that had ever happened to her. There was nothing to stop her going to look for a job in Marsillac, was there? After all, Philippe *had* said to look him up if she was ever his way.

'Where are we going?' she asked Simon, belatedly realising that they were cruising along the main road.

'I'm booked into a hotel about twenty miles from here. I'm sure they'll be able to find you a room for tonight.'

'I don't think I'd be able to afford the kind of hotel you're likely to stay at,' said Polly dubiously.

'I'll pay for your room.'

'I can't let you do that!' she protested.

'Don't be silly, Polly,' he said irritably. 'You told me yourself you haven't got any money. Do you think I'm going to leave you sitting by the road in the middle of the night with only a few francs in your pocket?'

'You could take me to Nice. I'm sure I could find a cheap hotel just for tonight.'

'I'm not driving round Nice at this time of night,' said Simon unhelpfully. 'It's not even in the right direction.'

Polly shifted uncomfortably. 'I just don't think you should be paying for my hotel room. The whole point of me coming to work in France was to prove to Dad that I could cope perfectly well by myself. I don't want to be dependent on anyone.'

'For God's sake, Polly, we're only talking about one night! It's partly my fault that you lost your job, anyway.'

'No, it isn't.' Polly turned in her seat to look at him in concern. 'It wasn't you who told Mrs Sterne that we were engaged. She was just looking for an excuse to sack me, in any case.'

'Still, she might not have been so angry if I'd told her right at the beginning that we knew each other.'

'Oh, well, it's too late now,' said Polly. 'I've been thinking about things, and I'm not sure it won't turn out to be for the best after all. It was a crummy job at the best of times, and maybe being sacked was just what I needed to find myself something better. It won't be quite the same as seeing the job through to the end, but as long as I spend the summer working in France I'll have proved myself to Dad.' She yawned again. 'I'm a great believer in fate.'

Simon glanced at her and shook his head at her casual attitude. 'Well, I'm a great believer in being sensible, so I suggest you stop making a fuss and let me take you to the hotel. You can have a good night's sleep, I'll settle your bill and you can think about what you're going to do in the morning. How does that sound?'

'Well…'

'If it makes you feel any better, I'm not giving you any choice in the matter,' he told her brusquely. 'I've done enough travelling for today, and I just want to get to the hotel and get some sleep myself. I certainly wouldn't be able to do that if I knew that I might have to tell your father that I'd dropped you off in the middle of Nice with all your carrier bags and absolutely no idea of where you were going, what you were going to do or how you were going to live in the meantime.'

'If you put it like that…' said Polly gratefully.

'I do. Tell yourself that I'm being selfish if that's what you want.'

Polly didn't think that Simon had ever been selfish.

Sensible, yes. Smugly superior, often. But selfish? No, he had never been that.

Even as a boy of eleven, acutely embarrassed by the adoration of a four-year-old, he had patiently put up with her tagging along behind him. Polly still cringed when she remembered how she had asked him to marry her in a loud voice in front of everybody. Any other boy would have crushed her with a jeering refusal, but Simon had been too kind to do that. Enduring the laughter and teasing of the others, he had patted her head and said that he would.

'Thank you,' she said simply, wondering if he knew that she was referring to more than just his offer to settle her hotel bill. 'I'll repay you when I can.'

Simon glanced at her. 'The best way you can repay me is by not arguing about it any more!'

'Yes, Simon. Certainly, Simon. Whatever you say, Simon.'

Simon had to laugh. 'Meekness doesn't suit you, Polly!'

Polly was taken aback by the way the laughter transformed his face, warming the formidably austere features, relaxing the severe line of his mouth and doing very strange things to her breathing. Had Simon always looked like that when he laughed?

'Some people are never satisfied!' she said, and was horrified to hear the breathless note in her voice.

She must be more tired than she had thought to start noticing things like Simon's mouth, to start wondering why she had never noticed before.

Much more.

CHAPTER THREE

'WE'RE not staying *here*?'

Polly jerked bolt upright as she read the sign blazoned over the hotel's entrance. She had been almost asleep when the car had crunched over the thick gravel to draw up outside the imposing front door, but she was wide awake now!

'Yes.' Simon pulled on the handbrake, as if it were the most natural thing in the world to book into a hotel so exclusive and expensive that Polly knew she couldn't even afford to *imagine* the bill. 'Helena and I often stay here on our way to La Treille. I booked a room for us both some time ago, so I hope they'll be able to find another one for you.'

'I hope they'll let me in,' said Polly, only half joking. 'They've probably never seen a plastic carrier bag in there!'

Simon turned round to regard the pile on the back seat with disapproval. 'I don't know why you can't use a case like anyone else,' he said, irritated as always by the state of chaos Polly seemed to carry around with her.

'I had a proper bag, but its zip broke,' she explained defensively. 'I would have bought another one, but I was waiting until I'd been paid, and I was so angry tonight when Mrs Sterne sacked me that I just had to shove my things into whatever I could.'

Simon sighed. 'I suppose it's too much to hope that

you'd put all your overnight stuff into one bag so that we don't have to have the whole lot brought in?'

'What do you think?'

Sucking the air through his teeth, Simon got out of the car. Why did Polly have to be such a *mess*? 'They can send someone out to bring them all in. If you think I'm going to trail in there laden down with all your rubbish, you've got another think coming! We'd better go and find you a room first, in any case.'

He set off up the steps before Polly's plaintive call made him stop and turn. 'Now what's the matter?' he asked in exasperation.

'I can't get my shoes on!' Polly had swung her legs out of the car and was trying to squeeze her toes into one of the shoes, but her feet were rubbed raw and so swollen by then that she couldn't imagine ever being able to wear them again.

'Haven't you got any others?'

'Somewhere.' She looked doubtfully at the clutter of bags on the back seat, but Simon was tutting impatiently at the bottom of the steps.

'Look, you might as well just come as you are. You look such a mess anyway that I don't suppose the fact that you're barefoot will make much difference!'

'Charming!' muttered Polly, manoeuvring herself gingerly to her feet. Typically, Simon had parked so that his door was right next to the steps, but she had to walk all the way round the car, yelping as the gravel dug into the soles of her poor feet. 'Ouch! Ouch! Ow-w-w!'

'For God's sake!' snapped Simon. His shoes crunched as he strode back over the gravel to Polly, who was leaning against the bonnet for support and screwing up her face in exaggerated grimaces of agony.

'I've never known anyone make such a *fuss* about walking a few metres!'

'Easy for you to say,' said Polly sulkily. 'You're wearing shoes and your feet aren't cut to ribbons! Look!' She lifted her foot to display the angry red marks where her shoes had rubbed against the soles and sides of her feet.

Simon had no intention of inspecting Polly's feet. It was obvious that there was going to be only one way to shut her up. Sighing, he put an arm under her knees and the other around her back, and lifted her up. 'Put your arm around my neck,' he ordered, and Polly was so stunned to find herself in his arms that she obeyed.

His body was rock hard, his arms like steel around her, and she swallowed, uncomfortably aware of him as he carried her over to the welcome smoothness of the stone steps. At five foot six and generously built, Polly was by no means a lightweight, but Simon carried her with ease.

'Thank you,' she muttered, ridiculously shy all of a sudden.

'Anything to shut you up,' said Simon, practically dumping her on her feet. He was more disturbed than he wanted to admit by Polly's soft, warm weight. He'd been irritated by her chaotic lifestyle, and she had seemed so much the familiar annoying Polly that it was unsettling to discover that there was nothing annoying and certainly nothing familiar about the feel of her in his arms. One hand had brushed her breast as he'd picked her up, the other could still feel the smoothness of the skin behind her knees.

'Let's go and find you a room,' he said brusquely, and set off up the steps without waiting for her.

Polly forgot her momentary awkwardness as she

walked into the hotel lobby. It was huge and furnished
with what she recognised as immaculate taste. She had
never been anywhere that shrieked elegance and ex-
pense in quite the same way, and she gawked openly
as she limped over to join Simon at the reception desk.

'This is *so* cool!' she whispered to him as he greeted
the receptionist, whose eyes flickered over her with
some surprise. Very conscious suddenly of her crumpled clothes and lack of shoes, Polly decided her only
option was to brazen it out and smiled sweetly back.

Simon launched into French too fast for Polly to follow, and a long discussion ensued, accompanied by
much shrugging of shoulders and shaking of heads.
Things didn't seem to be going that well, judging by
Simon's increasingly grim expression. 'What's the
problem?' Polly asked at last, bored of just standing
there.

'They haven't got a spare room,' Simon told her in
a clipped voice. 'There have been no cancellations and
the hotel is absolutely full. I thought they might be able
to squeeze you in somewhere, but they haven't got so
much as a broom cupboard.'

'Oh.' Polly had forgotten her earlier reluctance to
rely on Simon. The hotel looked so clean and luxurious
and welcoming, and now that she was here the thought
of trailing around for a hotel that she could afford herself at this time of night was more than unappealing.

She looked at Simon, who was frowning abstractedly
down at the desk. 'Can't I sleep with you?' she asked.

Simon's head jerked round. *'What?'*

'There's no need to look as though I've made an
indecent proposal,' said Polly, a little affronted by the
horrified expression on his face. 'You've got a room,
haven't you? Don't singles often have two beds?'

'I dare say,' said Simon dryly, 'but in this case there's only one. I was expecting Helena to be with me when I booked,' he reminded her.

'Oh…so it's a double bed, then?'

'Yes.'

'Well, I don't mind sharing,' Polly offered.

Simon's horrified expression had changed to one of deep suspicion. 'Share?'

'I'll bet the beds in this place are big enough to sleep six people, let alone two,' she said, having reached the point when she would do anything rather than start again when she was tantalisingly close to a shower and clean sheets. 'And, anyway, I don't know why you're looking so po-faced. It's not as if we haven't slept together before as children.'

'It may have escaped your attention,' said Simon with a careful lack of expression, 'but we're not children any more.'

Polly waved that aside. 'I don't see that it matters,' she said, conveniently forgetting how she had felt when he had lifted her up and held her against his chest. 'It's not as if either of us are going to have any trouble keeping our hands to ourselves, is it?'

Simon sighed inwardly. He really did *not* want to get into bed next to Polly. The memory of how it felt to hold her was still disturbingly fresh in his mind, and it wasn't likely to fade if she was lying right beside him in the dark. But what else was he going to do with her? It couldn't be that much of a problem, could it? This *was* Polly. She might have a much more tempting body than he had realised, but Simon was sure she could be relied upon to exasperate him so much that he would soon forget everything except how long it would take to pack her off back to her father.

'Don't worry about another room,' Polly said brightly to the receptionist, making up Simon's mind for him. 'I'll sleep with him.'

Wooden-faced, the receptionist glanced at Simon, who gave in and nodded briefly. 'She'll sleep with me.'

Polly was even more impressed by the room than she had been by the lobby. 'This is fabulous!' she said, leaning over the balcony and whistling at the sight of the swimming pool shimmering in the moonlight below. 'Do you often stay in places like this, or were you just trying to impress Helena?'

Simon looked down his nose as he loosened his tie. 'I don't need to impress Helena,' he said curtly.

Not any longer, anyway. Helena, he remembered, had been a hard woman to impress in any case. She would never have carried on like Polly, who was still wandering around the room, exclaiming as she opened cupboards and bounced on the bed, oohing-and-aahing at the simplest of facilities. Anyone would think she had never been in a hotel before, Simon thought, unable to decide whether he was amused or irritated by Polly's naive pleasure in discovering luxury for the first time.

Their luggage was delivered a few minutes later. Polly put a hand over her mouth to stop herself giggling at the contrast between her array of battered, bulging carrier bags and Simon's neat black case. Simon just shook his head in despair and slipped a generous tip to the expressionless porter.

'I suppose you realise you've ruined my reputation here? They probably think I've picked you off a street corner somewhere!'

'If you always come on holiday with a case like that, I'm sure they think you're much too uptight to do any-

thing so exciting!' she retorted, dropping to her knees
so that she could rummage through her belongings in
search of toothbrush, toothpaste and eye-make-up re-
mover. 'Honestly, it's only a few bags!'

'A few!' Simon threw himself into a chair and
watched Polly pull everything out of the bags and spill
them over the floor. 'I think they're breeding,' he said,
eyeing them with distaste. 'I'm sure there are more here
now than there were before! Are you sure you need all
this stuff?'

'Of course I do—aha!' She broke off as her fingers
closed over the hairbrush. Sitting back on her heels,
she flourished it triumphantly. 'Don't tell me Helena is
one of those women who manage to look immaculate
when they only ever have a clutch bag with them?'

Simon tried and failed to imagine Helena travelling
with an assortment of plastic bags, but the idea was
just too incongruous. In fact, it was pretty hard to picture Helena at all, he realised with a slight frown. If
he really concentrated, he could manage an impression
of cool elegance, but her features were blurred compared to the vividness of Polly's face and the dancing
lights in Polly's blue eyes.

'Can I have a shower?' Polly climbed to her feet and
stretched, and for some reason Simon found himself
remembering again the feel of her body beneath his
hands. He looked away with a scowl.

'If you promise to tidy up this mess when you get
back,' he said gruffly.

She just waggled her fingers at him as she disappeared into the bathroom, and he was left staring at the
door where her image seemed to linger long after she
had gone. He could hear the shower running, the sound
of her humming tunelessly, and was shocked to dis-

cover how vividly he could imagine her standing there, with water streaming over her body.

Abruptly, Simon got to his feet. If he had had any sense, he would have let Polly assure him that she was fine and kept on driving. It was his own fault for succumbing to the temptation to tease her. If he hadn't done that, he would never have been dragged into that party, never have had to pretend that he was engaged to Polly, never have had to take her away from the ghastly Martine Sterne. He could have had a relaxing meal on his own and spent a quiet night in a calm, peaceful room. Instead of which, he was irritated and unsettled and on edge.

Prowling moodily around the room, Simon kicked one of Polly's bags aside. She had only been in the room a matter of minutes and already it was transformed from an elegant apartment to a jumble sale. The chaos exasperated him—almost as much as the fact that he couldn't ignore the faint scent lingering on the air or the shimmer of her vibrant presence around him.

'I could get used to this kind of life!' When Polly burst out of the bathroom some time later, Simon was standing by the window, shoulders hunched, scowling down at the serene view. 'Look, fluffy robes!' She twirled round so that he could admire the full, luxurious effect. 'Isn't it gorgeous? There's one for you too. Do you think we get to keep them?'

'I doubt it.' Simon hoped she couldn't hear the absurd dryness in his voice. Unprepared, he had turned only to find the breath clog in his throat at the sight of her. Her thick blonde hair hung damply to her shoulders, and she was all long legs and glowing skin and dancing blue eyes. And beneath that soft, thick robe she was undoubtedly naked.

'Shame.' Polly did another twirl only to slow and then stop, arrested by the strange look in Simon's eyes. 'What's the matter?' she asked uncertainly.

'Nothing.' Simon cleared his throat. 'I think I'll have a shower myself.'

When he emerged from the bathroom in his turn, Polly was sitting cross-legged on the bed in a long T-shirt. Her head was bent and her newly dried hair hung down, hiding her face as she brushed it vigorously. She had made an effort to clear the bags to one big pile, but the room still managed to look as if a tornado had blown through it.

Muttering to himself as he picked his way across the room, Simon looked at her absorbed in her grooming and wondered what his lungs had been playing at. There had been no reason for his breath to stop just because she had put on a towelling robe. This was just Polly.

So she had matured a bit—OK, a lot—but she was still the spoilt, irresponsible, maddening Polly he had always known. If he hadn't been tired and irritated, he would never have noticed that somewhere along the line the long-legged adolescent had turned into a woman. The fact that he *had* noticed had made Simon even crosser, and perversely he blamed Polly for distracting him. Deep down, he knew that it wasn't entirely her fault, but it was certainly easier to be irritated by the old, infuriatingly insouciant Polly than to think about how disturbing the new Polly might be if he let her.

With a final stroke of the brush, Polly tossed back the mane of hair and looked mischievously up at Simon. 'I was just wondering if I should ring Mum,' she said. 'She would be so thrilled to know that I was spending the night with you!'

The fact that she seemed to be able to make a joke about it when he had been thrown off balance by the whole prospect only made Simon frown all the more. He frowned. 'I should think that's the last thing she wants to hear!'

'Oh, come on, Simon! You must know her one dream is for me to marry you, and your mother's not much better. They've never got over the way you accepted my proposal of marriage when I was four. Whenever they get together, they play "wouldn't-it-be-lovely-if...?", especially now that Emily's married and Charlie's engaged.'

'I'm sure they've realised by now that that particular dream isn't going to come true,' said Simon, throwing his shirt and trousers over the back of a chair. 'They only have to remember the parade of your boyfriends so far to see that your taste—if taste is the right word!—runs to jolly, rugby-playing types who are all beef and no brain.'

As a description of most of her boyfriends, it was unfortunately close to the mark, but Polly had no intention of giving Simon the satisfaction of admitting it. 'Maybe my taste has changed,' she said loftily, still brushing her hair. 'Philippe's not at all like that.'

'He's not your boyfriend either,' Simon pointed out unfairly.

'No,' Polly admitted with a sigh, 'but I'm allowed to dream, aren't I? Do you believe in love at first sight?'

'No,' said Simon.

Of course he didn't. He wouldn't. 'I think I fell in love with Philippe the moment I saw him,' she told him dreamily. 'I used to count the hours when I knew that he was coming to visit. I've never met anyone so attractive. All my boyfriends have been just that— boys—but Philippe's a real man. It's not just that he's gorgeous-looking. He's so cultured and assured and charming. All he has to do is smile at you, and you feel like a million dollars!' She heaved a reminiscent sigh. 'I wonder if I'll ever see him again?'

'I'd have thought you had more to worry about than Philippe Ladurie,' snapped Simon, revolted by all the gush. It was typical for Polly to fall for a pretty face, of course! 'The last time I saw him, he was fully occupied with a luscious redhead.'

'Oh, *her*,' said Polly gloomily. 'She was after him all evening.'

'Judging by the way she was wrapped round him, she obviously caught him,' said Simon dourly. 'If I were you, I wouldn't waste any more time thinking about Philippe Ladurie, Polly. He's out of your league.' He turned and opened his case with a snap. 'You'd be much better off thinking about something useful—like what you're going to do tomorrow.'

'Can't I think about it in the morning?' she pleaded. 'I can't do anything about it tonight, and something's bound to turn up.'

Simon grunted, unconvinced by her optimism as he pulled his shirt over his head and tossed it over the lid of his case. Polly found herself looking at his bare back as he stood there dressed only in a pair of pale blue boxer shorts, and the hand holding the hairbrush stilled and then lowered.

She had never noticed Simon's body before. If anyone had asked her to describe him, she would probably have said that he had rather a wimpish build, but there was nothing wimpish about those broad shoulders. In fact, now that she came to look at him properly, there was nothing wimpish about him at all, she realised in surprise.

His legs were straight and strong, and she could see the muscles corded at the back of his thighs. His back was smooth and somehow solid-looking, tapering from his shoulders to lean hips. Polly remembered how hard his body had felt as he'd lifted her across the gravel, and she had an insane urge to go over and lay her palm against his back, to feel the compact strength of the muscles ripple beneath his warm skin.

Unaware of her scrutiny, Simon turned and Polly hastily resumed brushing her hair, bending her head to hide the sudden surge of colour in her cheeks. He clicked his tongue as he saw her still fussing with her hair.

'Haven't you finished grooming yourself yet?' he asked with an irritable look, throwing back the cover and getting into bed. 'I've never known anyone spend so long just brushing their hair.'

Helena probably never had to brush her hair, thought Polly. She had the kind of hair that stayed perfectly in place all day. It probably stayed in place all night, too.

Scrambling up, Polly wished that she hadn't thought about Helena going to bed, because that meant remembering that she usually went to bed with Simon, just as *she* was about to do. Well, not *just as*, of course. Presumably Helena and Simon did more than lie side by side, which was all that she was going to do…wasn't it?

She cleared her throat, stupidly self-conscious about getting into bed beside him now that it had come to the point. 'I'll...er...just go to the loo,' she said and fled into the bathroom.

Sharing a bed with Simon had seemed such an obvious solution to the problem when she'd been standing in the hotel lobby, but it wasn't quite so easy now. If only she hadn't noticed what a nice body he had. Not as nice as Philippe's, of course, but still...nice. It felt all wrong to notice something like that about Simon.

Polly eyed the sofa on her way out of the bathroom. Perhaps she should offer to sleep there? But she had been so casual about the prospect of sharing a bed with him that she could hardly change her mind now. She would never hear the end of it if Simon guessed that she felt the slightest bit nervous.

Anyway, she wasn't nervous, Polly told herself firmly. She had absolutely no reason to be nervous. She was just being ridiculous. All she had to do was share an enormous bed with someone she had known all her life. It was only for a night, after all. What could be so difficult about that?

Nothing, Polly decided, but it didn't stop her switching off as many lights as she could before she walked over to the bed. In the solitary glow of the lamp beside the bed she could see Simon lying on his back with his hands behind his head. Polly was annoyed to notice that he looked utterly relaxed. The thought of sharing a bed with her obviously didn't bother *him*!

Well, it didn't bother her, either. Polly marched over to the bed, clicked off the lamp and got briskly in beside Simon. It was a wide bed and there was no danger of touching him, but she was still very conscious of him lying only an arm's reach away wearing only boxer shorts.

'This is the last place I imagined I would be sleeping

tonight when I woke up this morning,' she said into the darkness to cover her momentary unease.

She heard Simon sigh. 'It wasn't exactly top of my agenda either.'

'I hope Helena doesn't decide to surprise you by turning up after all,' Polly went on brightly, determined to prove that she really wasn't nervous. 'You might have a bit of explaining to do if she found you in bed with me!'

'I don't think that's very likely,' said Simon.

Barely repressing a shudder, he remembered that last nasty scene with Helena. She had made the mistake of issuing an ultimatum, and her fury when she'd discovered that he didn't take kindly to ultimatums had taken Simon by surprise. He had always thought of Helena as cool and controlled, but there had been absolutely nothing cool about the woman who had screamed and cried and thrown things.

Not that he had any intention of telling Polly that Helena was the last person who was likely to surprise them tonight.

'Yes, but what if she did?' persevered Polly. 'What would you say?'

'I'd simply explain the situation,' said Simon, irritation creeping into his voice. 'Helena would understand. She's met you, after all.'

Polly sat up. 'What do you mean by that?'

'Helena saw what you were like at Emily's wedding,' he reminded her.

'I was just having a good time,' she said, instantly on the defensive. 'Helena's trouble is that she doesn't know how to enjoy herself.'

'Of course she does. She's just capable of enjoying herself without downing a vat of champagne, making a complete fool of herself on the dance floor or causing grievous bodily harm in the scrum for the bouquet!'

'That was just one day,' said Polly a little sullenly, although it was almost a relief to find that Simon was as annoying as ever. 'I'm not always like that.'

'Maybe not, but I don't think Helena would ever feel that she needed to be jealous of you,' said Simon, and Polly bridled.

'Why not? It's not beyond the bounds of possibility that you might be attracted to me, is it?'

'That's not the point,' he said after only the tiniest of pauses. 'I'm not saying that you're not a pretty girl, but I've never thought of you as anything but John and Frances's daughter, and Helena knows that,' he finished so firmly that he even convinced himself.

Faintly dissatisfied, Polly lay back down. 'I suppose it's the same for me,' she said, settling herself more comfortably under the cover. 'I never thought of you as anything except Emily and Charlie's brother. I wonder what it would take to make us think of each other differently?' she mused, quite forgetting that she had spent most of the evening getting used to seeing Simon in a different light.

Simon didn't answer. He was hoping that she would shut up and go to sleep, but Polly was still hyped up. There had been a time in the car when she could easily have fallen asleep, but, now that she had passed the peak of tiredness, the events of the evening were still buzzing around her brain.

'We'd probably have to kiss or something,' she was rambling on. 'It might be hard to keep on thinking of you as the same old Simon after that. What do you think?'

'I've no idea,' said Simon, sounding bored. 'Why don't you try it and find out?'

His question brought Polly up short. She hadn't been really thinking about what she was saying, almost talking to herself, and now Simon's cool suggestion was like walking into a wall in the dark.

Turning his head on the pillow, Simon could make out her disconcerted expression and he smiled sardonically. 'Doesn't seem like such a good idea now, does it?'

As soon as the words were out of his mouth, he knew they were a mistake. Polly wouldn't be able to let a challenge like that pass, and of course she couldn't. 'Yes, it does,' she said, as he had known that she would. 'Let's try.'

'You try,' said Simon, cursing himself for a fool. 'Personally, I'm happy to go on thinking of you as I've always done.'

He didn't want to kiss her, Polly realised, miffed. Not only that, he didn't think that she would dare kiss him without any encouragement. 'All right, I will,' she said defiantly.

'Well?' sighed Simon as she hesitated. Hoping to put her off, he spread his arms in mock invitation.

Polly bit her lip, but it was too late to turn back now. Awkwardly, she edged across the mattress until she was leaning over him. They were very close. She could feel his chest rising and falling steadily as if to emphasise that he wasn't in the slightest bit excited by her nearness. Suddenly she felt rather silly.

'Are you sure you don't mind?' she asked doubtfully.

'Just get on with it, Polly,' said Simon, disguising his own awareness of her beneath a show of profound irritation. 'I don't know about you, but I'd like to get some sleep tonight.'

Up to that point Polly had been planning a quick peck just to prove that she wasn't scared, but Simon's sarcasm put her on her mettle. Shifting until she could look right down into his face, she lowered her head slowly. As she did so, a swathe of blonde hair fell forward over her shoulder and Simon felt its softness tickle his cheek moments before Polly's lips brushed his mouth tantalisingly and everything seemed to stop.

Polly felt that unexpected jolt of sensation at that first fleeting touch of their lips, too, and she froze, staring down into Simon's eyes. Part of her urged her to draw back and leave it at that. You've proved your point, it said sensibly. Get out before you make a real fool of yourself.

But there was something stronger, drawing her down, drawing her on, and without being aware of making a decision Polly kissed Simon again. It was a proper kiss this time, one that went on and on and acquired a life of its own. Polly had forgotten that this was Simon. She knew only that his mouth was warm and persuasive and that her lips seemed to belong against his. It felt so right, *frighteningly* right; it felt wonderful.

Helpless against the intense pleasure that gripped her, Polly sank down onto Simon and his hands rose as if of their own volition to twine in the long blonde tresses and hold her head still so that he could kiss her back. The kiss went on and on, became deeper and more urgent until Simon rolled her beneath him and Polly wound her arms around his neck, gasping at the feel of his body and the searing excitement of his hands hard against her.

Simon's fingers were sliding possessively up her smooth thigh beneath her T-shirt when he realised dimly that if he went any further he wouldn't be able to stop. It was enough to make him pause, and then, as the reality of what they were doing dropped sickeningly into place, he withdrew his hand with an effort and lifted his head.

For a long, long moment they stared at each other in the dim night light, their breathing ragged and loud in the jarring silence.

'Well?' said Simon almost harshly at last. 'What do you think?'

'Think?' echoed Polly with difficulty. She moistened her lips. She couldn't think of anything except how good it had felt. Her senses were afire, her body thumping, and she was having trouble concentrating. 'Think?' she said again blankly.

'Now that you've kissed me, do you think of me differently?' he reminded her.

Memory rushed back like a slap in the face, and Polly wrenched herself away from him. God, what had she been *doing*? It was supposed to have been a brief kiss just to show Simon, and instead...instead... Instead it had been something quite different. Polly swallowed. Who would have thought that Simon—*Simon!*—would kiss like that?

She was trembling with reaction, unable to believe how quickly their embrace had burned out of control, how abruptly it had ended. It hadn't felt like kissing Simon at all, but the sardonic undercurrent to his question sounded all too familiar. He obviously didn't think of *her* any differently, Polly realised with a surge of resentment. If it hadn't affected him, she was damned if she was going to admit that it had had any effect on her either!

'Not really,' she said unsteadily and untruthfully.

'Good,' said Simon with an infuriating lack of re-action. 'Now that we've cleared that up, perhaps we can get some sleep?' he went on, and, calmly turning on his side so that he had his back to her, he settled himself comfortably and to Polly's fury went straight to sleep.

CHAPTER FOUR

POLLY woke to an empty bed the next morning, and for a while she lay blinking at the sunlight and wondering why the curtains looked so unfamiliar. It always took a little time for Polly's brain to engage in the mornings, and images from the previous evening swirled drowsily in her head without making much sense.

There was Philippe, smiling and telling her that she was pretty, and Martine, looking cross, and then there was Simon—

Polly's eyes flew open as memory clanged back into place. Simon! Now that she had started remembering, the memories came thick and fast: facing Martine down with her hand tucked in Simon's arm, being carried by Simon over the gravel, *kissing* Simon.

Polly jerked upright, heart lurching at that last memory. Please, let it be a dream, she prayed, but she knew that it wasn't. She could remember the feel of his lips and his body and his hard hands sliding up her thigh with devastating clarity. Vivid imagination she might have, but she couldn't have made up the response still tingling through her.

When Simon had turned on his side, she had lain awake for what seemed like hours, burning from his touch, cursing herself for being such a fool. It had been a stupid thing to do, kissing him like that. It had been stupid to even *think* about it, but she had been restless, not yet ready to sleep, and at the time it had seemed like an interesting question.

The only trouble was that she had lied when she had told Simon the answer. She *did* think of him differently now. It was impossible not to. Polly had turned her head on her pillow and looked at Simon sleeping with his back to her. His head had merged with the darkness of the pillow, but she'd been able to make out the line of his shoulder in the darkness and the faint sheen of his skin. She'd known what that skin felt like and she'd been gripped by a terrifying urge to slide over and touch her mouth to his shoulder, to put her arms around him and press herself against that hard, strong body...

The sound of the bathroom door opening jerked Polly back to the present and her heart hammered uncomfortably as Simon appeared, wiping his face with a towel.

'About time,' he said with an indifferent glance at Polly sitting bolt upright in bed. 'I thought you were never going to wake up.'

'What time is it?' To her horror, Polly's throat was so tight that her voice came out as a pathetic squeak.

Simon picked up his watch from the bedside table. 'Half past eight,' he said, and she eyed him covertly as he fastened the strap around his wrist. Part of her wanted to be reassured that it was the same old Simon. He certainly *looked* the same. In what was obviously a major concession to holiday mode, he had left off his tie and was wearing a green short-sleeved shirt and pale chinos. His brown hair was damp from the shower, but the austere lines of his face were just the same as always.

Polly could almost persuade herself that nothing had

really changed until she made the mistake of looking at the stern mouth, and the fingers that were deftly fastening the watch strap and the memory of the kiss which she was trying so hard to suppress rose up and swamped her.

Simon might look the same, but things didn't feel the same. They didn't feel the same at all.

Not that Simon seemed to notice the change in atmosphere. 'I'm going to have some breakfast downstairs,' he said, and there was nothing in his eyes or his voice to suggest that he had ever rolled her beneath him and kissed her until she'd gasped with pleasure last night. 'Are you coming?'

'I'll just have a quick shower,' said Polly, relieved to discover that her voice sounded almost normal again. 'I'll see you downstairs.'

Standing under the shower, Polly gave herself a stern talking-to. Last night obviously hadn't meant anything to Simon, so it was important not to overreact. She had been tired and hadn't been thinking straight, that was all. Everything seemed different in the dark. Perfectly ordinary noises were magnified in the middle of the night to sinister sounds, and it was the same with kisses. The devastating embrace she remembered existed only in her imagination, Polly decided. In reality, it had just been a little peck on the lips. It clearly hadn't been enough to bother Simon, so there was no need for it to bother her either.

By the time she pulled on white jeans and a cropped top, Polly had convinced herself that there was no reason to feel the slightest bit awkward. She had been making a fuss about nothing. They would be going their separate ways today, in any case. There was no big deal.

True, her confidence faltered when she went out onto the terrace where the tables were laid charmingly for breakfast under the vines, but it was only for a moment. Simon was sitting at a corner table, reading a French newspaper, and as Polly looked everything about him seemed suddenly very definite. The lines of his nose and jaw, the set of his head, the long, competent fingers holding the paper all stood out as if in relief, and when he glanced up and saw her watching him his eyes were very cool and clear. In spite of herself, Polly felt her heart do a funny little somersault, but she recovered quickly.

It was only Simon, remember?

Simon folded his newspaper as she sat down opposite him. 'I've ordered coffee and croissants for you,' he told her. His manner was so much what it always had been that Polly felt a rush of relief. She really *had* been imagining things. Nothing had changed at all. Everything was fine.

'Wonderful,' she said with a beaming smile. 'I'm starving!'

She hadn't eaten anything since a rushed lunch the day before, she realised, and the fat, buttery croissants that arrived were some of the best things she had ever tasted. She ate three and then sat with her hands cupped around a bowl of milky coffee, looking contentedly out at the blue Mediterranean sky. She could relax now that she knew that things hadn't changed between her and Simon after all.

Simon watched her, conscious of a growing sense of irritation. It was typical of Polly to get an idea, to push it until everyone else gave in and then sit back and pretend that nothing had happened! He couldn't get the feel of her, so warm and sweet and vibrant, out of his mind. Turning away from her last night had been one of the hardest things he had ever done.

He had tried so hard to dismiss the kiss, and he had almost succeeded until he had come out of the bathroom and seen Polly sitting up in bed, wide-eyed and temptingly dishevelled, blonde hair tumbled and T-shirt slipping off one shoulder. He had got out of the room as soon as he could, but it seemed as if she was determined not to make things easy for him. Looking at her now, smiling dreamily, licking the croissant crumbs off her fingers, was playing havoc with his self-control! She had obviously put the whole business out of her mind.

Simon scowled down into his coffee. She might at least have the decency to appear embarrassed!

'I asked about flights at reception,' he said abruptly. 'I could get you to the airport for the eleven-thirty plane.'

Polly looked blankly back at him. 'Plane?'

'I think the only sensible thing is for you to go home.'

'I can't do that!'

'I'll buy your ticket, of course.'

'It's not that.' Polly didn't know whether to be amused or angry at Simon's determination to pack her back to England. 'I said I was going to spend the summer in France and that's what I'm going to do. I'm not slinking home just because of one setback,' she told him, lifting her chin. 'I can still hardly string two words of French together, and I told Dad I'd be fluent the next time I saw him. I *can't* go back yet, Simon.'

Simon didn't answer directly. Instead he nodded at the bag she had slung over the back of her chair. 'Have you got your purse with you?'

'Yes.'

'Get it out and show me how much money you have.'

Biting her lip, Polly opened her purse and emptied the contents onto the table, so that she could count it out slowly. 'Forty-eight francs,' she admitted reluctantly when she had finished.

'How long do you think that's going to last you?'

Polly tucked the notes away and swept the coins into her palm. 'I'll get a job,' she said defiantly.

'Doing what?'

'Look, what's with the interrogation?' she grumbled as she dropped the coins back into the purse and clicked it shut. 'There must be masses of things I could do...washing dishes, waitressing...all sorts of things,' she finished rather lamely.

'I'm sure the possibilities are endless,' said Simon, not even bothering to hide his sarcasm, 'but, in the meantime, you've still got to have something to live on while you find someone prepared to employ you. Even if you *do* get a job, you won't get paid until you've worked for a while. How are you going to pay the rent? What are you going to eat?'

'I'm not entirely alone in France, you know.' Polly shook back her hair. The more Simon pointed out how impossible it was for her to stay, the more determined she was to do just that! 'I've got contacts.'

'Like who?' he asked sceptically.

'Well...like Philippe Ladurie, for instance. He said I could go and see him whenever I wanted,' she added with pride, not that Simon looked at all impressed.

'Was this before or after his sister sacked you for telling a pack of lies?' he enquired.

Polly ignored that. 'Look, he even gave me his card.'

She rummaged in her bag for the precious bit of card with Philippe's name embossed across it and handed it across the table to Simon.

'Marsillac...' He read the address, grey eyes suddenly keen.

'It's not that far from here, is it?' said Polly hopefully.

'A couple of hours' drive.' Simon sounded preoccupied. Recollecting himself, he gave Polly the card back. 'You realise that people give out cards like this the whole time? It doesn't mean anything.'

'I know, but still, I'm sure Philippe wouldn't mind if I asked him if he could recommend me for a job. He was really nice when we talked last night.'

Simon sighed at the tone of her voice whenever she talked about Philippe Ladurie. He didn't understand how women could make such fools of themselves over a man like Philippe who seemed to have nothing to recommend him but a handsome face and a smug manner.

'So, what's your plan?' he asked, resigned to the fact that Polly wasn't going to do the sensible thing and accept a ticket home.

'All I have to do is get myself to Marsillac and contact Philippe,' said Polly crossly. 'How much more of a plan do I need?'

'What if he's not there? He might still be fully occupied with his redhead.'

'Then I'll get a job by myself,' she said. 'Marsillac doesn't sound that big a place.' The more she thought about it, the more she liked the idea. She was bound to bump into Philippe sooner or later, wasn't she? Even seeing him from a distance every now and then would be better than nothing.

Simon was still being exasperatingly practical. 'It'll cost you more than forty-eight francs to Marsillac from here.'

'I can always hitch,' said Polly. She didn't like the idea, but she was damned if she was going to let Simon talk her out of staying in France, money or no money.

Somewhat to her surprise, Simon didn't immediately shoot down the idea. He was rubbing his chin pensively as he considered the idea that had glimmered in his brain when Polly had shown him Philippe's card. Was it possible that Polly's situation might turn out to be very convenient after all?

Frowning slightly, he tried to work out whether the advantages of his plan would outweigh the very definite disadvantages, most of them answering to the name of Polly Armstrong. But it *could* work...

'I'm going to Marsillac,' he told her slowly.

About to drain the last of her coffee, Polly put the cup back down in surprise. 'You are?'

'It's the local town. La Treille is only about five miles from there.'

Polly was a little puzzled by the sudden change in Simon's attitude, but she couldn't let an opportunity like that go by. She looked at him hopefully. 'You wouldn't like to give me a lift, would you?'

'I might,' said Simon. 'On one condition.'

'What sort of condition?' she asked blankly.

'That you be my fiancée for the next two weeks.'

Polly started to laugh. 'No, go on, what is it really?'

'That's it,' said Simon calmly. 'I'll take you to Marsillac if you promise to act as my fiancée for a fortnight.'

Her smile faded as she stared at him. 'You're not serious?'

He met her look coolly. 'Don't I look serious?'

'But...but...*why*?'

'I'll explain.' Simon glanced round to catch a waiter's eye and signalled an order for more coffee with the barest lift of his finger. Polly, who would have been reduced to waving wildly before she got the waiter's attention, was at once impressed and obscurely resentful at the way Simon managed to make everything look so easy.

Unaware of her thoughts, Simon turned back to Polly. 'I said that I was here on holiday, but it's more than that,' he began. 'I'm trying to set up a deal—a crucial deal to my company's future. We've done well in North America and the Pacific Rim, but we really need a stronger base in Europe itself, and we've found a company that complements our interests perfectly. Now all we have to do is convince their Chief Executive that a merger is in their interests as well.'

'Hold on!' said Polly, waving a hand in front of his face. 'I want to know why you suddenly need a fiancée, not a lecture on economics!'

'If you'd just listen, I'd tell you,' said Simon, irritated at the interruption. 'The Chief Executive of the other company is called Julien Preucel, and he's married to Chantal, who just happens to be an ex-girlfriend of mine. It was Chantal who pointed out that my company and Julien's have a lot in common when she heard that I was investigating potential mergers on the Continent.

'My people have done some investigation into the structure of the company and so on, but I thought it would be a good idea if Julien and I met informally at first to see if we could work out a deal on a personal basis, and I invited him and Chantal to La Treille for a couple of weeks' holiday.'

'These are the friends you're going to meet?' she twigged at last.

Simon nodded as the waiter arrived bearing a pot of fresh coffee. Polly sniffed appreciatively and refilled their cups. 'I still don't see what all this has to do with me,' she said.

'I'm just getting to that.' Simon watched her pour milk into her coffee and stir it with a spoon. This was the difficult bit. 'When I spoke to her on the phone, Chantal warned me that Julien is inclined to be very jealous of our friendship. She and I had a very close relationship, and we stayed close after Chantal went back to France. She's a wonderful person,' he went on, his voice warming with affection. 'Beautiful, gentle, intelligent…Chantal's one of the nicest people I know.'

Beautiful. Gentle. Intelligent. Polly tried to imagine Simon describing *her* like that, and was conscious of a faint tweak of jealousy. She had never heard him talk about anyone with that kind of warmth before. Chantal must be very special.

'If she's that marvellous, why didn't you marry her?'

Simon had been turning a spoon between his fingers, but he looked up at the edge in Polly's voice. 'That's none of your business,' he said coldly. 'The point is that Julien resents the fact that Chantal and I are still close. One of the main reasons for inviting them to stay was to show Julien that he has absolutely no reason to be suspicious of me. At the time, of course, Helena was going to be there as well. I thought that if he saw that I was in a settled relationship with another woman, he would stop wondering if I was still interested in Chantal and we could get down to business. As it is…'

'Helena is in London and he's going to think that you and Chantal have cooked up the idea between you so that you can be together?' Polly finished for him.

Simon nodded. Polly might be exasperatingly silly at times, but she wasn't that slow to get the point.

'Helena was going to come,' he said, picking his words with care. After listening to Polly raving on about Philippe, he didn't feel any more inclined to let her know the true state of his relationship with Helena. 'But an urgent job came up at the last minute, and, rather than cancel the whole visit, I thought I would just come on down and see how things went.'

Polly sipped her coffee and wondered if Helena's job might be just an excuse. Even a superwoman like Helena might be allowed to be jealous if Simon went on about Chantal to her in the same way. Now that she thought about it, Polly did vaguely recall her mother being very depressed because Simon had a wonderful French girlfriend and various rumours about a possible engagement had floated around for a while, although nothing had ever come of it.

Had Chantal broken his heart? It was hard to imagine Simon being that romantic, but his voice certainly sounded different when he talked about her. Did he still harbour a secret passion for her? If that were so, Polly didn't blame Helena for not letting herself be dragged into the affair.

'It was you that gave me the idea in the first place.' Simon's voice broke into her musings, and she looked up, startled.

'I did? What idea?'

'That ridiculous story you made up for Martine Sterne,' he reminded her. 'Remember, how I chased all over France after you and dragged you out to the pool and begged you to marry me?'

'Oh, yes.' Polly grimaced. In the cold light of day she'd wondered how she had the nerve!

'Neither Chantal nor Julien know Helena,' Simon went on. 'All they know is that I'll be there with my girlfriend. There's no reason why *you* shouldn't be Helena. And, since it's not for real, we might as well go one better and tell them that we're engaged. That's bound to make Julien realise he can relax. What do you think?'

'I think it's a crazy idea!' said Polly roundly. 'Nobody's going to believe that we're engaged.'

'Why shouldn't they? Martine Sterne did.'

'Not really, and anyway, Chantal obviously knows you much better than Mrs Sterne. She's bound to know that I'm not your type, to say the least!'

Simon shrugged. 'If I say that I'm in love with you, I don't see any reason why she shouldn't believe me, and all you need to do is wear a ring and look suitably adoring. What could be easier than that?'

'Lots of things,' said Polly tartly. 'Being with you doesn't exactly make me feel adoring!'

'You can act, can't you?'

'Not that well!'

Cool grey eyes looked directly into blue. 'You gave a pretty good performance last night,' Simon reminded her unfairly. 'And an even better one this morning unless you really have forgotten that kiss!'

To her chagrin, Polly felt her face grow hot. 'Oh, that,' she said, wanting to sound dismissive but horribly afraid that she sounded embarrassed instead. The memory of the kiss shimmered between them, too vivid to ignore, too disturbing to discuss.

'Yes, *that*,' said Simon at his most ironic. 'If you kissed me like that occasionally in front of Julien, he'd soon realise that he had no need to be jealous and he could relax.'

Polly's eyes slid away from his. 'What exactly are you suggesting?'

'I'm offering you a straightforward deal. If you agree, I take you to Marsillac and you spend the next two weeks convincing Julien that you're engaged to me. At the end, I'll pay you enough to spend the rest of the summer in France doing whatever you want to do. If you want to hang around Marsillac drooling over Philippe Ladurie, that's up to you, but you'd be able to travel around and put some money aside to go home when you were ready.'

Polly absorbed that. 'And if I don't agree?'

'Then we'll say goodbye now with no hard feelings. I'll entertain Julien and Chantal on my own and you can see how far you get on forty-eight francs.'

'It's not much of a choice, is it?'

'It's a better choice than either going home or washing dishes for a living, isn't it?'

Polly swirled coffee around in her cup. 'What else would I have to do, apart from looking adoring?'

'Just be the hostess. I don't have any help in the house, so there'll be shopping and cooking to be done, but we can share that, and I'm sure Chantal will give a hand too. It's meant to be a holiday, after all. You can relax and do what you like as long as you don't give Julien any reason to suppose that we're not in fact madly in love with each other.'

'And how do I do that?'

'I wouldn't have thought it should be that difficult,'

he said, unconcerned. 'All you have to do is not argue
and kiss me now and then for effect.'

'Will…will we share a room?' A touch of colour
tinged Polly's cheeks, and Simon lifted an eyebrow.

'Julien might think we had an odd kind of relationship if we didn't,' he said coolly. 'We shared a bed
last night, and it didn't seem to be a problem then.'

Maybe not for him, Polly thought sourly. But she
couldn't say that to Simon without admitting that she
had been shaken by the effect the kiss had had on her,
and that would never do!

'I won't take advantage of you, if that's what you're
worrying about,' Simon added with one of his ironic
looks.

Polly tilted her chin. 'I wasn't worrying about that—
although if I was Helena I might be! Won't she mind
when she finds out that we've been…?'

'Sleeping together?' Simon finished for her as she
hesitated.

'In a manner of speaking,' she said stiffly.

Simon looked out across the terrace. He could tell
Polly the truth about Helena, he supposed, but it might
not be a bad thing if she thought that he was still firmly
committed to another woman. Getting into bed next to
Polly for the next two weeks was the major drawback
to the plan which otherwise seemed to solve so many
of his problems.

It wouldn't have been so bad if it hadn't been for
that kiss last night which had got dangerously out of
control, and which was proving disturbingly hard to
push from his mind. No, much better for Polly to understand that as far as he was concerned she was just
a stand-in for Helena. She was obviously obsessed with
Philippe Ladurie, so if he made it clear that he was

equally involved with Helena there would be no room for misunderstandings and things would be easier all round.

'Helena won't mind,' he said to Polly. 'She knows how important this merger is to me, and that I'm prepared to do whatever it takes to see that it goes ahead.'

'Even if that means sleeping with me?' said Polly tartly.

'Even that.' Simon finished his coffee and put the cup back down into its saucer with a decisive click. Now that he had embarked on this story, he had better make it convincing. 'Helena and I have a very special relationship,' he went on, looking Polly full in the eye. 'We understand each other.'

Or he had thought they did, until Helena had switched out of the blue from a high-powered lawyer to a woman demanding marriage and babies. Taken aback, Simon had suggested they put the idea on hold for a while, but once Helena had started laying down ultimatums the end had been in sight. Now or never, she had said, and he had chosen never.

'We've got the ideal relationship,' he told Polly, sensing that she was less than convinced. 'We live the same kind of life, want the same kind of things. Helena is smart, funny and very practical. She'd be the first person to see how convenient it is that you're available to step into her shoes for a short while.'

Polly regarded him somewhat sourly. Chantal was beautiful and gentle, Helena was smart and funny and practical—Simon's highest accolade!—but *she* just got to be convenient!

'Well?' said Simon at last. 'Will you do it?'

Would she? Polly thought about it as she stirred her coffee. She was more thrown than she wanted to admit by the extraordinary offer he had made. It seemed so unlike Simon! Part of her was unnerved by the whole idea of spending a fortnight with him, *sleeping* with him. If it hadn't been for that kiss last night, she wouldn't have hesitated. Now, though, the prospect seemed fraught with potential awkwardness.

On the other hand, she didn't really have much choice. She might pretend to Simon that she was sanguine about the idea of heading out into the unknown with barely enough for a coffee and a *croque-monsieur*, but it wasn't that appealing. She could look on acting as Simon's fiancée as just another job. Awkward it might be, but surely it would be better than washing dishes?

'All right,' she said, making up her mind abruptly. 'I'll do it, but I've got a couple of conditions of my own.'

'What are they?'

'Number one, you're not to tell my parents. I know they think I'm a bit dippy, but I'm not, and it's really important to me to prove to them that I can do what I set out to do. If they hear that I got sacked, they'll think that I can't manage on my own and that you're just giving me a job out of pity.'

Simon looked amused. 'I might feel responsible for you, but even I would draw the line at sharing a bed with you out of pity! I've got no intention of telling your parents anything, and I won't be telling anyone else either—especially not Emily! She would never let us forget it if she knew we'd spent all that time together at La Treille.'

'God, no, we mustn't tell Emily!' Polly agreed in horror. Emily was one of her best friends but the first thing she would ask would be if Polly had kissed

Simon, and then she would ask if she had enjoyed it
and *then* what would Polly say?

'What's the second condition?'

'I won't pretend to be Helena. I'd never be able to
convince anyone that I was a hot-shot lawyer and, anyway, I don't think I'd feel comfortable about it. If
Chantal knows Helena's name, you'll just have to say
that you've fallen in love with me instead.' She forced
a smile. 'That should be a challenge for you! How's
your acting?'

For an answer, Simon reached across the table and
took hold of one of her hands. Turning it over, he lifted
it to his lips and pressed a warm kiss into her palm.
'Have I ever told you how beautiful I think you are,
Polly?' he asked, looking deep into her eyes.

A wave of colour swept up Polly's face. Her hand
burned where his mouth had touched her skin and dis-
maying little shivers were vibrating up her arm. She
tried to tug her hand away, but Simon only tightened
his clasp, curling his fingers around hers. Polly was
very aware of their warm strength, sure that she could
feel every line and crease, every whorl on his finger-
tips.

She was finding it absurdly hard to breathe as well.
She wanted to laugh and look away, but she couldn't
take her eyes from his. She had never noticed before
how thick and dark his lashes were, or what a startling
contrast they made to those piercing grey eyes.

'My acting's good enough, I think,' said Simon
softly, still holding on to her hand. 'How's yours?'

The words hung in the air like a challenge.

Polly swallowed. Simon wasn't taking this seriously,
and she had to convince him that she wasn't either. If
she backed down now, he would know that she had

lied, that she *did* think of him differently, and Polly didn't think she could bear that. Much better for him to believe that she could be as casual about all this as he could.

Polly's eyes dropped to Simon's mouth, remembering how right it had felt to kiss him last night, and all of a sudden it was easy. As if it were the most natural thing in the world, she leant across the table and kissed the corner of his mouth before letting her lips drift enticingly to his. And Simon leant in to meet her, and somehow the teasing brush of lips against lips became a kiss so intoxicatingly sweet that Polly had to force herself to break away.

Inwardly shaken, she sat back and across the table her eyes met Simon's. His expression was utterly unreadable. Polly just hoped that hers was the same.

'It's only acting,' she said, astonished at how level her voice sounded. 'I'll manage.'

CHAPTER FIVE

'Is THIS it?' Polly peered through the windscreen as Simon drew up in front of an old farmhouse half hidden in the shade of old plane trees and gnarled olives.

Simon lifted an eyebrow at the surprise in her voice. 'What's wrong with it?'

'Nothing. It's very pretty,' said Polly, looking at the curved pink roof tiles and faded shutters. Pots of geraniums stood on the rustic forecourt, bright splashes of colour against the dry stone walls. 'It's just not what I was expecting, that's all.'

'Oh? What did you think it would be like?'

'I'm not sure. Houses are supposed to reflect your personality, aren't they?' she said as she got out of the car. The air smelt wonderful, hot and heady with jasmine, mimosa and the thyme that she was crushing underfoot. 'I've always pictured you living somewhere very functional,' she went on, following Simon to the front door. 'You know, lots of clean lines and no clutter.'

'There *is* no clutter,' said Simon, inserting a key into the lock. 'And it's going to stay that way. I don't want you spreading your mess all over the house,' he added severely. 'I'm not going to spend the next two weeks wading through carrier bags!'

Polly pulled a face at his back as he opened the door. In contrast to the warmth and colour outside, the hall was dim and cool and welcoming, with thick stone walls and flagstones on the floor.

77

They had spent the morning arguing about everything from music to chocolate and from politics to the real reason dinosaurs became extinct as they drove along the long, straight French roads with the sunlight flickering between the poplars. It was so much like being with the Simon she remembered of old that any awkwardness after that kiss over the breakfast table had completely dissolved.

Not that Simon gave any sign that he felt in the slightest bit awkward. Once he had got his way, he had been all brisk practicality, ordering her up to the room to get ready, paying the bill, packing her unceremoniously into the car while he'd shoved her collection of bags into the back seat with a number of trenchant comments about her inability to live out of a briefcase.

He would never have treated Helena or Chantal like that, Polly thought resentfully. They would have been handed tenderly into the car. Simon would have fussed around them, opening doors, carrying their no-doubt minimalist matching luggage, making sure they were comfortable. He wouldn't have told *them* to get in and stop complaining!

'What do you think?' Simon led her into a spacious living area, furnished with the kind of stylish simplicity Polly had only ever seen in glossy magazines. Everything was immaculate, every picture perfectly placed, every fabric carefully chosen for the maximum effect.

Polly looked around her critically. 'I prefer a more lived-in look myself,' she said. 'I can't imagine lying on a sofa eating ice cream and watching telly in here, for instance.'

'That's because it's meant to be a place where you

have intelligent conversation,' said Simon, nettled by her lack of appreciation.

'You don't have to be uncomfortable to have a good chat.' Polly threw herself onto one of the long, cream sofas and swung her legs up. 'Where do you and Helena slob out?'

She stretched luxuriously, and Simon found himself remembering the feel of her body beneath his hands. Frowning the memory aside, he pointedly pushed Polly's feet off the end of the sofa. 'We've got better things to do than slob out,' he said sharply as he straightened one of the cushions she had dislodged.

'What, like making sure that all the cushions stand to attention?'

Simon's mouth tightened. 'Helena and I like to enjoy each other's company in comfort. Neither of us can relax in the squalor that seems to be your natural habitat!'

'So I'm not the tidiest person in the world,' said Polly, unconcerned. 'I'd rather live comfortably with a bit of mess than spend my time feeling tense about whether I could put my feet up on the sofa or not!'

Wandering over to the glass doors, she peered outside. 'What's out here?'

'The terrace.' Simon unlocked the doors and pushed them open so that she could step out into the dappled shade of a luxuriant vine. Unlike the cool elegance of the room inside, the terrace was a riot of colour, with flowers spilling out of their pots and tumbling over the warm stone.

'Oh, dear,' said Polly in mock concern. 'You're going to have to do something about the gardener, Simon. He's been getting sloppy while you've been away. Look at these flowers growing any old how! Shall we just push these pots back into a straight line and prune all the plants so that they look nice and neat and tidy?'

'Very funny,' said Simon coldly.

Grinning, Polly walked down the worn steps into the sunlight and found herself in a wild garden, surrounded by olive trees with gnarled trunks and silvery-green leaves. Cicadas shrilled in the rough grass below, jasmine scrambled over a wall and the air was heady with the scent of mimosa. Polly turned up her face to the sun and closed her eyes with a happy sigh.

'Now *this* is my kind of place!'

Simon watched her dourly from the terrace. How could he have forgotten how exasperating she was? He had a nasty feeling that his brilliant idea of getting her to stand in for Helena might turn out to be a bad mistake. If he felt like this after a morning with Polly, what was he going to be like at the end of two weeks?

Now she was plucking a sprig of lavender from a sprawling bush, lifting it to her face, extravagantly breathing in its fragrance. Just as Simon was deciding that she was getting more irritating by the minute, she looked up at him, her generous mouth curving into a smile that was part apology for teasing him before.

'It's beautiful,' she said.

The sun was glinting off her hair and burnishing her bare shoulders. She was wearing jeans and some kind of sleeveless top, and Simon had a sudden, uncomfortably vivid image of what it would be like to run his hands down her arms and feel the warmth of her flesh.

'Come and see upstairs,' he said brusquely.

A sunny landing opened into a series of bedrooms and bathrooms, all decorated with the same effortless style as the rooms downstairs.

'And this is my room,' said Simon, opening the last door. 'Or perhaps I should say *our* room!'

Polly walked primly past him. It was a lovely room, all natural textures and neutral colours, striped by the sunlight shafting through the louvered shutters, and dominated by a big, cast-iron bed.

Simon's bed. It gave Polly an odd feeling to think of him lying there. That was presumably the bed where Helena slept too when she was here, the bed where they made love. Did he kiss Helena the way he had kissed *her* last night?

Something shifted in the pit of Polly's stomach, and she looked quickly away. She wished she hadn't thought about that stupid kiss. Now she was going to have to think about what it would be like to climb into bed next to Simon tonight, knowing just what it was like to feel his mouth exploring hers, his hard body pressing her down into the mattress, his hands sliding under her T-shirt.

Not that there was any need to worry. Simon had made it obvious that he had no interest in repeating the experiment. He had spent all day going on about how marvellous Helena and Chantal were, and it was pretty clear that if the past and present women in his life shared anything, it was the fact that they were completely and utterly different from *her*.

Simon patently didn't find her in the least bit attractive. And that was a good thing, Polly reminded herself hastily. She didn't find him attractive either. Not *very* attractive, anyway.

She slid him a covert glance under her lashes. He really wasn't good-looking at all—certainly not compared to a man like Philippe, for instance—but there was *something* about him, she had to admit. At first glance, his face was unremarkable, but a second look made you realise that there was something formidable about the set of his jaw and the stern line of his mouth. Understated, he might be, but that air of cool competence and quiet, contained strength could be considered very attractive.

If you liked that sort of thing.

Which, of course, she didn't.

Still, Polly wished she didn't know how compactly muscled his body was, or how persuasive those cool lips, or just how close he was going to be when she got into that bed tonight.

Swallowing at the thought, she wrenched her gaze away from the bed and went over to the window so that she could push open the shutters and look out over the tops of the olive trees to the rolling hillsides of lavender.

'What a wonderful view!'

'There's another room if you want to sleep in there until Chantal and Julien come,' said Simon dryly.

Polly stiffened. If he insisted on being so damned perceptive, he might at least have the decency to keep it to himself! She couldn't accept the offer now, could she? It would only make him think that she was nervous about sleeping with him, and she couldn't have him thinking *that*.

'I don't think it's worth it for two nights,' she said instead, turning with a shrug that she hoped looked suitably casual. 'As you said, it wasn't a problem sleeping together last night, so we might as well carry on like we did then.'

'I hope you're not planning on carrying on exactly like you did last night,' said Simon, deliberately seeking refuge in sarcasm. He was strangely unsettled by the sight of Polly in his bedroom. He had hoped that bringing her up here would remind him of how little she fitted into his life, but somehow she managed to look much more at home in here than Helena had ever done.

'Or do I have to prepare myself to be kissed every night?' he went on unfairly, wanting to underline the point that he stood in no danger of taking that disturbing kiss seriously, but unsure of whether it was Polly or himself that he had to convince.

'Of course not.' Polly flushed and folded her arms defensively in front of her. 'I don't think either of us want to repeat that particular experience.'

'Don't we?'

Polly's heart missed a beat and she looked uncertainly across the room. He was joking...wasn't he? Simon just looked back at her, his expression impossible to read.

'You're not going to tell me you enjoyed it?' she said, horribly conscious that the light tone she aimed for had fallen sadly flat.

'Didn't you?' he countered.

Polly bit her lip. She could deny it, but he was bound to know that she was lying. She *had* enjoyed it. It might make her cringe to admit it, but it was true.

'It was OK as kisses go,' she said bravely. 'But it was just a kiss.' She swallowed. 'You're still the same old Simon to me, and I'm no different from the Polly you've always known.'

'I don't know about that,' said Simon, considering her. 'I didn't recognise anything in the Polly who kissed me last night.'

'It takes two,' Polly pointed out, goaded into forgetting her embarrassment. 'You kissed me too, if you remember!'

'True, but only because you were doing it so enthusiastically that it seemed rude not to join in!'

Polly eyed him resentfully. 'Well, you needn't worry. I won't put you through it again!'

'I'm afraid you're going to have to,' said Simon in a cool voice. 'We'll need to kiss occasionally to convince Julien and Chantal that we're suitably lover-like.'

'You haven't been exactly lover-like so far,' said Polly tartly, thinking of the way he had bundled her into the car that morning. 'You'd better get in a bit more practice before they arrive.'

To Simon, the words sounded like a challenge. 'You think I need to work on my technique?' Stung by the apparent ease with which she could dismiss the kiss that had lingered with such uncomfortable clarity in his mind, and angry with himself for not being able to treat it with the same indifference, he walked over to where Polly stood by the window, took hold of her waist and pulled her almost roughly towards him.

'W-what are you doing?' Polly was caught off-guard, her hands coming up instinctively to press against his chest.

'Practising,' he said, looking down into her startled and apprehensive blue eyes, his own cold and clear. 'You were the one who said that I needed it.'

'I didn't mean…' The breath snarled in her throat as he lifted his hands to cup her face.

'Didn't mean what?' asked Simon softly, his eyes on her mouth.

Polly moistened her lips and tried again. 'I didn't mean…' But his thumbs were drifting almost absently along her jaw, unaware that the merest brush of his fingers was sending tiny tremors over her skin. Her heart was thumping against her ribs, and her voice died as she stared dumbly up at him, aware that she could move away, but held still and breathless between his palms by the look in his eyes.

'Didn't mean this?' he suggested, and bent his head to touch his mouth to hers.

Afterwards, Polly thought of all the things she should have done. She should have stepped back, or pushed him away, or turned it into a joke, but she didn't do any of those things. Instead she closed her eyes and parted her lips in a tiny sigh, as if she had been waiting for him to kiss her like that ever since he had turned up on the Sternes' doorstep.

Simon's fingers drifted over her face to tangle in the soft blonde hair and hold her head steady as he deepened the kiss. His lips were tantalising, gentle and yet demanding, and so enticing that Polly could feel the last pitiful remnants of resistance dissolving beneath a tide of sheer pleasure.

The sun pouring through the window seemed to drench her in a golden light. Something about the touch of Simon's lips had heightened every one of her senses, so that she was intensely aware, not just of the feel of his hands and the taste of his mouth, but of the warmth of the sunshine on her skin, and the hot, scented air and the frantic whirr of the cicadas below the window.

There was a deep thrill building inside her, spiralling up from the base of her spine to twine around her heart, holding her captive beneath the delicious onslaught of his lips. Hardly aware of what she was doing, Polly leant into Simon, sliding her arms around his neck, and when he succumbed to the heady temptation of her and gathered her closer she murmured with pleasure.

Simon heard her murmur, and the possibility that she might have been protesting registered dimly in his brain. What was he thinking of? His senses were reeling and it took every ounce of will-power that he had to lift his head and slowly release her.

'Was that better?' he asked, appalled to hear the ragged note in his voice.

Polly blinked at him, her eyes a deep, dazed blue. His question seemed to come from a long way away, filtering slowly down into her brain. With it came the brutal shock of reality. Reality wasn't, after all, that golden enchantment, but Simon with a quizzical look in his eyes and a cool, detached question.

Carefully, she disengaged herself, leaning back against the windowsill for support. Take it lightly, she told herself, furious with herself for melting into a puddle the moment Simon touched her, angry with him for not knowing the effect he had on her and aghast to discover that a part of her—not just a big part but a *terrifyingly* big part—just wanted to fling herself back into his arms and beg him to go on kissing her.

'Yes, it was better.' It wasn't quite the cool tone she was hoping for, but in her current state Polly thought she was doing pretty well to string any words together at all.

'Practice makes perfect?' To her relief, Simon stepped back. He had himself well under control again, and his casualness infuriated Polly. He might at least have the common decency to look as if it had had more effect on him than drinking a cup of tea!

'That's what they say,' she managed. At least her voice wasn't wobbling all over the place now.

'Perhaps we should keep practising?'

The ironic gleam in Simon's eyes was enough to

bring Polly's chin up. He needn't think that she was going to let on that she was still shaking inside and her bones felt so weak that she didn't think she could stand up straight.

'Perhaps we should,' she agreed, her eyes bright and blue with challenge. 'If we kiss every day as a matter of routine, we should be able to do it quite naturally when it comes to doing it in front of Julien and Chantal. We'll be so used to it that we won't need to make a big deal out of it. Kissing will just be something we take for granted.'

Simon couldn't imagine ever taking a kiss like that for granted, but he was secretly impressed by her cool. 'Don't you think that's rather a dangerous game, Polly?'

'No.' Polly was gaining confidence. She would show him! 'It's not as if either of us finds the other attractive. I mean, you're in love with Helena, and I'm in love with Philippe. Kissing each other is just something we have to do as part of the pretence. It's not something we *want* to do.' If she said it often enough, she might even believe it. 'I just think it would be more convincing and easier for us both if we treated it as something we've rehearsed so often that we can do it without thinking.'

Simon studied her thoughtfully. There might even be something in what she said. 'So you think we should treat kissing as a sort of daily chore?'

'Exactly. Like buying bread or washing up.'

Simon thought about kissing Polly every day. A chore? Or something far more disturbing than that?

'When do you want to start?' he asked, unable to think of a way to back out of the situation. 'Now?'

Polly longed to have the sang-froid to say yes, but

she didn't trust herself. She was still humming with the effect of that last kiss and she wasn't sure that she would even stay upright without the support of the window-ledge. 'We've done today,' she said, her eyes sliding away from his. 'Tomorrow will be soon enough.'

'Has it escaped your notice that the bedroom is fully equipped with wardrobes and drawers?' Simon came into the kitchen irritably the next morning, a tattered carrier bag hanging distastefully from one hand. He shoved it in the bin and let the lid clang shut.

Polly winced and held her head. 'Has it escaped your notice that I have a terrible hangover?'

Unable to face a shopping expedition to stock up the previous afternoon, he had taken her to the restaurant in the village, a small, unpretentious place with a reputation for excellent food.

Not that Polly remembered that much of what she had eaten. In spite of her brave words, she had become increasingly nervous as the evening had approached. It was all very well to talk about taking kissing him for granted and treating it as a chore, but it was different when she had to lie next to him in the dark and remember how it had felt.

In the restaurant, she had quickly gulped down a couple of glasses of wine, and it had worked. After a while she had relaxed, and had even enjoyed the evening. It was a nice change to go out with someone she didn't need to impress. Usually when she went out on dates, she spent her time running to the Ladies to see whether the nervous blotches had faded on her throat, or to check whether her mascara was smudged, and she either laughed too much and too loudly or was so anxious to make a good impression that she hardly said a word.

With Simon she hadn't had to worry about any of that. She could just be herself, and even getting into bed with him hadn't been a problem when they had finally got home.

This morning, though, Polly's head was thumping and her mouth felt horribly dry in spite of the multiple cups of tea she had made herself this morning to try and rehydrate. Swallowing two paracetamol, she looked blearily at Simon.

'I don't know what you're grumbling about. I knew you'd make a fuss, so I put everything away.'

'Odd how your idea of "putting away" and mine can be so completely different, isn't it?' he said sarcastically. '*I* think putting away means unpacking my clothes and putting them in the wardrobe. You, on the other hand, apparently think it means strewing them around the room, covering every available surface with rubbish and chucking anything you can't find an immediate home for onto the floor!

'And that's just the bedroom!' he went on. 'The bathroom looks like a bomb hit it in the night.'

Simon was in a bad mood. It was all right for Polly. She might have a hangover, but at least she had had a good night's sleep. She had staggered up to bed and snored peacefully all night, while he had been left to stare at the ceiling and wonder how he had let her invade his calm, ordered life.

He didn't like the way she argued with him and distracted him. He didn't like the air of turbulence that surrounded her even if she was sitting still. He didn't like the way she had turned apparently overnight into a woman he was finding increasingly hard to ignore.

And he couldn't stand her mess. She was incapable of closing a drawer. When he had gone into the bathroom just now, he had found bottles on their sides, tubes oozing lotions, jars of cream without their tops and talcum powder drifting everywhere. The tap had been dripping and a wet towel had lain in a heap on the floor where she had dropped it.

Tight-lipped, Simon had tidied up after her, only to discover that she had managed to turn the kitchen into a shambles as well. She was sitting at the table with tousled hair, surrounded by used tea bags, toast crumbs and half-empty mugs of cold tea. The sight of her made Simon remember Helena nostalgically. Helena was so neat and tidy and *restful* in comparison to Polly.

Removing the carton of milk and dropping the tea bags in the bin, Simon sighed and sat down opposite Polly. 'Have you written a list yet?' he asked, and she lifted her head from her hands.

'What for?'

'We're about to go shopping,' he reminded her testily.

'There's no point in a list,' said Polly. 'We need everything, so we might as well just see what there is in the market.' Gingerly, she tested her head to see if the paracetamol were having any effect yet. 'I don't believe in lists, anyway. There's something so…repressed…about them.'

'Efficient is the word you're looking for,' snapped Simon. 'You do realise that you're going to be feeding four people for the next couple of weeks, don't you? Helena would have planned a week's menu and drawn up a list of ingredients by now.'

'This is supposed to be a holiday, not a military campaign,' complained Polly. 'I don't see why you can't just relax and enjoy things as they happen.'

Simon looked down his nose. 'If you're organised, you get more time to enjoy things.'

'Huh! I bet you and Helena can't enjoy anything until you've added it to your list of things to do! How does it go…? Wake up, breathe, enjoy ourselves, go to bed…!'

Simon's mouth tightened. 'I might remind you that you're getting paid for these two weeks, Polly. I hope you're planning to do something to earn all that money!'

'I'm pretending to be in love with you,' she said with a morose look before she put her head back into her hands. 'What more do you want?'

'You agreed that you would act as a proper hostess. That means making sure that the beds are made, that the house is tidy, that there's something to eat whenever we need a meal.'

'That's being a slave, not a hostess,' Polly grumbled. 'I might as well still be working for Martine Sterne. At least I didn't have to kiss her!'

Simon bit back a retort. There was no point in arguing with Polly when she was in a mood like this. 'All right, *I'll* write the list.' He sighed, taking a pen from his shirt pocket. 'You go and get ready.'

'I am ready.' Polly lifted her head, affronted.

He looked over at her with raised brows. 'You don't think it would be a nice gesture to put some clothes on to go into town?'

'This is a sun-dress,' she said slowly and clearly, as if explaining a difficult concept to a child. Standing up, she gave him the benefit of a full-length view, not that there seemed to be much length involved, Simon reflected. The dress was very short and clung lovingly to her curvy body below narrow shoulder straps. 'It's the latest fashion,' she told him.

'There doesn't seem to be very much of it.'

Polly rolled her eyes at his disapproving expression. 'It's supposed to be short. That's the whole point. It shows off my legs.' She smoothed the material over her hips and looked down complacently at her legs. 'They're my best asset, so I have to make the most of them.'

'Your best asset? What rubbish!' Simon had found a bit of paper and was writing a list in a precise hand.

'They are!' Polly bridled. 'Everyone says that I've got great legs.'

'There's nothing wrong with them,' said Simon as he wrote. 'I'm just saying that they're not your best asset.'

'Oh, really? I didn't realise you were such an expert!' she said sarcastically. 'And what, in your considered opinion, *is* my best asset? And don't you dare say my personality, which is what Mum always says!'

He did look up at that. 'Believe me, Polly, your personality this morning is about the last thing that would spring to mind!'

'Well, what do *you* look for in a girl? What do you find most attractive about Helena, for instance?'

Simon's eyes dropped back to his list as he added 'jam' to it. '*Her* personality,' he said.

'I meant physically.'

He sighed. 'Her hair…her eyes. She's got beautiful skin, a wonderful figure. She's a beautiful woman, but I couldn't say that any one bit of her was "best". The whole point about attractiveness is how all the bits go together, surely?'

'I don't know about that.' Polly came round and perched on his side of the table, sticking out her legs as she considered them. 'If you were setting me up for a date with one of your friends, and you wanted to make *me* sound attractive, I bet you'd tell him about my legs first.'

'No, I wouldn't.'

'What, then?'

Simon tried to concentrate on his list, but it was hard with Polly sitting there, swinging those legs—and she was right, he had to admit. They *were* great legs. He wrote down 'fruit', 'cheese' and 'coffee', wishing that he could think of some way not to answer. He was taken aback by just how many things about Polly that he could describe as attractive: her scent, the fullness of her breasts, that shadowy hollow at the base of her throat, things he had never been aware of noticing before now.

Things he wished he hadn't noticed. Things he somehow couldn't admit to noticing, especially not to Polly.

'Well?' she prompted.

'You have a nice smile,' he said at last. He might easily have noticed her smile, Simon told himself, feeling oddly jarred. It would be much more difficult to explain why he had noticed intimate details like her perfume or the generous curve of her breasts, even to himself. *Especially* to himself.

'A nice smile?' echoed Polly, conscious of an inexplicable sense of disappointment. That was what people said when they couldn't find anything more interesting to say. 'Everyone has a nice smile,' she said accusingly.

Simon glanced at her. She wasn't smiling now. In

fact, she was looking positively grumpy, but he could picture her smile with unnerving clarity. He had never thought about it before that moment, but he knew *exactly* how her lips curved, exactly how her lashes tilted, exactly how the blue eyes gleamed with fun. God, he thought, shaken off balance. Anyone would think he had taken her for A-levels!

'Not everyone has a smile like yours,' he said as if the words had been forced out of him.

There was a moment of silence, oddly charged, and for some reason Polly felt her cheeks burn. A nice smile: it was hardly head-turning stuff as far as compliments went, and yet the fact that Simon had noticed it at all made it seem curiously intimate. She had been thrilled when Philippe had told her that she was pretty, but she hadn't felt unsettled the way she did now.

'Well, I'm glad you like it,' she said, striving to sound flippant, as if she had hardly noticed his comment, as if she hadn't been aware of that tiny pool of silence, as if she hadn't blushed like a fool. 'I think I'll stick with my legs, all the same. You know what they say—if you've got it, flaunt it!'

'You certainly seem to have taken that advice to heart today!'

Polly was almost grateful to him for his sarcasm, which restored the balance between them in a peculiar way. 'You never know,' she said, jumping from the table. 'If we're going into Marsillac, I might bump into Philippe, and I'd want to be looking my best if that happened.'

Simon gave an exasperated snort. 'You're not really in love with him, are you?'

'I'd love the chance to be. He's my dream man,' said Polly soulfully, not averse to another chance to underline the fact that Simon wasn't her type at all. Leaning over his shoulder, she tapped his bit of paper. 'Put him down on your list of things to get for me, along with a cure for my hangover!'

The blonde hair swung down, tickling Simon's cheek, and he was dizzily aware of her warmth, of her perfume drifting by him.

Pushing back his chair, he got abruptly to his feet and tucked the list away in his breast pocket. 'If you're that ready, Polly, we might as well go.'

CHAPTER SIX

'WHICH one do you like?' asked Simon as he leant forward to inspect the tray of rings that the jeweller had reverently placed on the counter.

'I don't know,' said Polly, dazzled by the choice. 'Shouldn't we just get the cheapest?'

'You're going to have to wear it for the next two weeks, so you might as well have one that you like.'

Still Polly hesitated. They were all so beautiful—and so expensive! 'Are you sure it's necessary? It does seem an awful waste to buy an engagement ring just for a fortnight.'

'Look, Polly, we've been through this,' said Simon impatiently. 'Announcing our engagement will be the crowning touch as far as Julien is concerned, and a few diamonds flashing on your finger will do more to convince him than anything else.'

'But what are you going to do with it afterwards?' she protested. 'If you're planning to give it to Helena, you'd better get one that you think that *she* would like, not one that I like. Our tastes might be completely different.'

They were bound to be, she thought with an inward sigh. Marvellous, beautiful Helena with her perfect skin and her slender figure wasn't going to like anything that scruffy, far-from-slender Polly would like, was she?

Simon was wondering whether it would be possible to find a more tactless gift for Helena than a used diamond ring. Briefly he allowed himself to imagine the scene, turning up on Helena's doorstep, explaining that he still had no intention of marrying her but tossing her an engagement ring that another girl had worn as a compensation prize.

'No, I don't think I'll be passing it on to Helena,' he said. His voice was so dry that Polly looked at him in surprise. 'Helena deserves a much more special ring than any of these,' he added hastily, before she started wondering why he was so reluctant to buy a ring for the woman he had told her he was in love with. 'I certainly wouldn't give her one that you had worn. You might as well keep it.'

'*I* don't want it!' Polly drew back, affronted at the implication that she was somehow not fit to touch anything deemed worthy of his precious Helena. 'I'd be terrified of having an expensive ring like one of these. I'd spend my whole time worrying about losing it.'

'Surely even you should be able to keep track of a ring if it's stuck on your finger?'

'Yes, but it wouldn't *be* on my finger, would it? I couldn't wear a ring unless it was a real engagement ring. And what would I say if Mum or Emily asked me where I got it?'

'Oh, all right, *I'll* keep it.'

Simon sighed irritably. He had had a trying morning shopping with Polly. His idea of shopping was to work methodically through a list and get the job done as efficiently as possible. Hers was to wander up and down the aisles in a haphazard fashion, picking up the most useless items she could find, changing her mind every five minutes about how much she needed and deciding that she had passed what she really wanted two aisles earlier.

It had been even worse in the market, where Polly had insisted on going to get the fruit and vegetables. Sublimely indifferent to Simon chafing at the bit, she had drifted from stall to stall, exclaiming over the cheeses laid out on straw mats, peering into barrels of olives, inspecting crates of glossy aubergines and fat tomatoes and pale, plump asparagus, and sniffing melons with a discerning air, without, however, buying anything. Only when she had completed a leisurely tour of every single stall in the market did she return to the first one they had passed, where she awarded her custom to the stall-holder on the grounds that he had the nicest smile.

A muscle was beating in Simon's jaw by the time they had finished. He practically frogmarched Polly back to the car where they packed everything away, but there was still the ring to get before he could recover his strength with some lunch.

'Can we just get on with it, Polly?' he said tersely. 'I don't want to spend all day in here.'

'Hmm...' Polly dithered over the rings until he picked up a band of rubies and offered it to her.

'Here, try this one. It goes with your eyes.'

'Ha, ha!' she said with a mirthless laugh, and then sighed. 'Don't tell me I look as bad as I feel?'

Why was it only Polly who could wind him up until he was boiling with exasperation and then disarm him utterly by making him laugh, even when he least wanted to? In spite of himself, Simon gave in again. 'You look a lot better than you did this morning!'

Polly turned back to the array of rings, dismayed to find that the laughter in his eyes had stopped the breath in her throat. What on earth was the matter with her? It was only Simon laughing.

'How is your hangover now, anyway?' he asked with mock solicitude.

'A bit better.' She concentrated fiercely on choosing a diamond solitaire and on breathing in and out. It couldn't be that difficult. She had been doing it perfectly easily for twenty-three years and there was no reason for her lungs to suddenly stop working now.

Picking out at ring a random, she tried it on her finger. 'It's a bit big,' she said lightly.

'What about this one?' Simon offered her a spectacular, square-cut sapphire. He glanced at her. 'This one really *does* go with your eyes,' he said slowly. He sounded taken aback, as if the thought had crept up on him unawares.

Polly found her gaze locked with his. She wanted to look away, to make some flippant comment, but she couldn't. They looked at each other, and something seemed to tighten in the air between them, something indefinable, something unfamiliar, something almost disturbing.

Confused, suddenly uncertain without knowing why, Polly managed to jerk her eyes away at last and struggled to remember what they were supposed to be talking about. 'I…I think a diamond would be more appropriate.'

Simon was grateful to her for breaking the contact. He stared down at the tray, making a show of inspecting the rings while he tried to blink away the image of Polly's deep blue eyes which for some reason seemed to be imprinted on his vision. Eventually, he succeeded in focusing on a striking band of sapphires and diamonds.

'We could compromise,' he suggested, and, without giving himself time to wonder whether it was a good thing to do or not, he took Polly's hand and slid the ring onto her third finger. 'What do you think?'

All Polly could think was that he was still holding her hand and that the feel of his fingers was sending an odd shiver down her spine. She made herself look at the ring. 'It's beautiful,' she said and risked another glance at him.

He was watching her with the same strangely unreadable expression. Polly was so used to seeing exasperation or mockery in his eyes that she wasn't sure how to react when they weren't there. Her gaze flickered away from his, but something drew it back and she found herself looking into his eyes as if she had never seen them before.

They were the same light, penetrating grey that they had always been, but somehow suddenly disconcerting. Polly could see the startling contrast of his dark lashes, the creases fanning out from their edges, the texture of his skin. Her heart was booming in her chest. She wanted to tear her eyes away, as she had done before, but she was held, pinioned by his odd expression, and all she could do was sit and stare at him and feel a trembling start deep inside her, as if she had suddenly found herself teetering on the edge of a cliff and didn't dare look down to see how far she might fall.

'It's a shame our mothers can't see us now, isn't it?'

It was Simon who broke the electric tension of the moment and, passionately grateful to him, Polly gave a shaky laugh. 'They'd be beside themselves, wouldn't they? Your mother would be straight off to buy a hat, and mine would be on the phone to the vicar before we had a chance to change our minds!'

'Lucky they're not here, then,' said Simon.

'Yes,' she agreed. 'Very lucky.'

She had a nasty feeling that she didn't sound as enthusiastic about their luck as she might have done, but Simon didn't appear to notice. His fingers tightened around hers. 'Do you really like the ring, Polly?'

He sounded as if he really cared whether she did or not. 'Yes.' Polly moistened her lips surreptitiously and made herself meet his eyes again. 'Yes, I do.'

'In that case, it's yours for the next two weeks.'

Just for two weeks. Polly looked down at the ring on her finger as Simon turned to agree the sale with the jeweller. She was conscious of a ridiculous sense of wistfulness. What would it be like if they were here for real, not because it was convenient to pretend to be engaged, but because they were in love and wanted to be together for ever?

There was no point in wondering that, though. Simon was never likely to be in love with her. She was too messy, he was too precise. She was too casual, he was too organised. They would drive each other up the wall.

Polly watched Simon signing the credit-card voucher. Her eyes rested on his mouth and a peculiar feeling that could even have been regret tiptoed down her spine. He couldn't even cope with a shopping expedition together, she reminded herself. All morning, she had felt him mentally comparing her with Helena who planned her menus and wrote lists and who deserved a really special ring.

It should be Helena sitting here, not her, realised Polly sadly.

'What's the matter?' To Polly's embarrassment, Simon turned without warning to catch her watching him with an expression that must have said far more than she wanted it to.

'Nothing,' she said, feeling the treacherous colour rise in her cheeks. 'I'm just hungry.'

Simon tucked the credit-card voucher in his wallet and slid it back into his pocket. 'Come on, then,' he said. 'Now that this particular chore is over, we can go and have some lunch.'

Outside, the light was glaring after the dimness of the shop, and Polly was glad of the excuse to shield her eyes with sunglasses. She wished Simon hadn't mentioned chores. It reminded her too uncomfortably of that crazy suggestion she had made yesterday about a daily kiss. That was supposed to have been a chore too. The prospect was churning at the back of Polly's mind. Perhaps Simon had forgotten about it, she thought hopefully.

They found a pavement table under the shade of some old plane trees in the main *place* where they could watch the world go by. Polly rested her arms on the table and looked at the bright light and the vibrant colours and the bustling square, and gradually regained her equilibrium as the atmosphere seeped into her.

So what if she wasn't really engaged? What did it matter if Simon was in love with a girl as boringly neat and organised as he was? The important thing was that she was in France, and, once these two weeks were over, the summer stretched enticingly before her. She would have money in her pocket, she would be able to travel around and have a good time, and she would prove to her parents that coming here had been exactly the right thing to do.

Simon finished giving their order to the waiter and turned back to see Polly gazing dreamily out at the *place*, her mouth curved contentedly. The sunlight through the trees threw dappled shadows over her skin, and the sight of her bare shoulders beneath those absurdly skimpy straps was enough to remind Simon that, beguiling as the dress might be, it had been worn in honour of someone else entirely.

'Are you keeping a lookout for Philippe?' he asked, surprised at the harshness in his voice.

'Philippe?' Polly was startled to discover a moment of blankness before she remembered who Philippe was. How could she have forgotten Philippe, of all people?

She had been watching a small boy trotting past with a baguette under each arm, and not thinking about anything in particular when Simon's voice had interrupted her, but she didn't have any objection to him thinking that she had been dreaming about Philippe. She had heard so much about Helena this morning that it wouldn't do him any harm to remind him that he wasn't the only one longing for these two weeks to be over.

'He might be back by now,' she told Simon casually. 'And this would be a good place to spot him if he does come into town.'

'What are you going to *do* if you do see him? Run over and throw yourself at his feet, or stop and tie yourself up in ribbon first?'

'No,' said Polly with dignity. 'I'll just go over and say hello, and explain that I'm working here.'

'I hope you're not planning on telling him exactly what your job is,' Simon warned.

'I'll have to,' she protested, sitting back in her chair. 'There's no point in letting him know that I'm here if he thinks that I'm engaged to you.'

Simon was unmoved. 'Too bad,' he said. 'You can tell him the truth or whatever you like after Chantal and Julien have gone, but until then it stays between the two of us. It was your condition, after all. It's not as if a man like Philippe is going to be interested in you, anyway,' he finished dismissively.

Polly shook back her hair. 'Stranger things have happened,' she said defiantly. The waiter was hovering, and she smiled her thanks as he put a plate in front of her. 'You should never underestimate the power of chemistry.'

'*Chemistry?*' Simon laughed scornfully, leaning back to make a space for his own meal.

She passed him the basket of bread. 'You know, that instant connection between a man and a woman. It doesn't matter how different you are if the chemistry is right. It's the basis of every successful relationship.'

'That's good coming from someone whose idea of a successful relationship is being given a business card!' he said snidely. 'As someone who knows what it's like to be in a successful relationship, as you call it, I can tell you that it's about compatibility and having things in common, not physical attraction.'

Polly banged the bread basket back down on the tablecloth. 'Like you and Helena, I suppose?'

'Exactly. Helena is bright, independent, focused and, above all, she's organised. She doesn't waste my time by being late for everything, she doesn't throw her clothes on the floor, she doesn't litter her things around my flat—'

'Don't tell me!' She cast him a sour look as she tore her bread. 'She *always* puts the top back on the toothpaste?'

'Yes, she does,' said Simon calmly. 'It's a little thing, but it's a symptom of the fact that she thinks like I do. That's why we get on so well together. We're perfectly suited in every way.'

So why had he been conscious of a sense of relief when Helena had stormed out? Simon frowned slightly as he picked up his fork. On the face of it, Helena was everything he wanted in a woman, but it was true to say that it had been a comfortable relationship rather than a passionate one.

'Maybe, but would you be in love with her if she wasn't beautiful as well?' asked Polly.

'I'm not saying physical attraction doesn't matter,' he said, avoiding answering her question directly, 'just that other kinds of compatibility are more important. Luckily, Helena and I have both.'

Well, bully for them! Polly poked crossly at her tomato salad. 'I think love is more romantic than that,' she said. 'I think it's about a room that feels empty when the person you love isn't in it. It's about your toes curling with happiness just knowing that they are. It's about knowing the instant you see someone that you want to spend the rest of your lives with them. I could imagine falling passionately in love and getting married the next day.'

The worst thing was that Simon could imagine her doing it, too. 'It's a terrible risk,' he said.

'Maybe, but I think that a marriage like that stands just as good a chance of succeeding as one where you've established what you both do with the top of the toothpaste and written punctuality and tidiness into the pre-nuptial contract! When I fall in love,' she told him grandly, 'it's going to be for ever!'

'What—like it was with Harry and Mark and Nick and all the others?'

'I didn't realise you'd been keeping track of my love-life,' said Polly with a frosty look. 'Anyway, I wasn't really in love with any of them. They were just boy-girl affairs. True love is something different, like a thunderbolt out of the blue.'

'Is that what happened when Philippe Ladurie handed you his business card?' asked Simon sarcastically. 'Funny, I was in the room, and I didn't notice any thunderbolts!'

'It didn't happen then,' she told him sweetly. 'It happened the first time I saw him.'

'Oh, for God's sake!' Simon tore savagely at his bread. 'You don't know anything about him other than the fact that he's handsome and has a sister who treated you like dirt.'

Polly patted her heart with a provocatively soulful look. 'I know what he's like in here!'

It would be just like Polly to do something stupid like embark on an affair with Philippe Ladurie, thought Simon, regarding her with exasperation. She would never be able to deal with a man like that, a man who, according to the accounts Simon had heard, was an inveterate womaniser, a playboy with no evident means of support for his idle and extravagant lifestyle, and much too old for her, to boot! If Polly *had* to fall in love, why couldn't she do it with someone sensible?

Like him?

Simon stiffened as the thought jumped unbidden into his mind, and he pushed it violently away. Of *course* not with someone like him! That really would be a recipe for disaster. Quite apart from anything else, they were looking for completely different things. He wanted compatibility, she wanted thunderbolts. She wouldn't get any thunderbolts from him!

For a brief moment, Simon's mind wavered as he remembered the electric excitement that had flared so unexpectedly between them when they had kissed, but

Polly was obviously looking for something much more than that. She was apparently still determined to make a fool of herself over unsuitable men, and, even if she did feel the same spark when they kissed, they would be lucky if they lasted a week before he strangled her as it was. She was utterly impossible to live with.

But that didn't mean that he wanted to see her hurt, and Simon was very much afraid that that was what would happen if she took up with Philippe Ladurie. It wasn't any of his business, he knew, but her parents had done so much for him since his own father had died that he felt a sense of responsibility for their exasperating but beloved daughter. He couldn't just let Polly throw herself into a disastrous affair without even making an effort to stop her.

Moodily, he wiped his plate with some bread. He had enough to worry about with the merger without having to worry about Polly as well.

On the other hand, there was no point in worrying about something that might never happen. The chances of a man like Philippe showing much interest in Polly were remote, after all. Not that she wasn't a pretty girl, but Philippe's tastes probably ran to rather more sophisticated women.

She might not even see him at all. Marsillac wasn't that small a place. Polly would sigh soppily over him for a week or two, but she would soon lose interest if Philippe showed no sign of appearing. The more he thought about it, the more Simon decided that he could relax. Polly's infatuation with Philippe was one problem he would probably never have to deal with.

He was wrong.

'Let's get some flowers,' said Polly as they walked

past a stall brimming with luxuriant foliage and brilliantly coloured blooms.

'We don't need any flowers,' Simon objected, but she ignored him, dragging him over to the stall and exclaiming at the size of the sunflowers.

'I know they're not on your precious list, but let's get some anyway. They'll make the house look nice for Chantal,' she coaxed.

'All right, one bunch.'

'Oh, don't be so miserable,' said Polly gaily, picking out a great bunch of cornflowers. 'We *are* supposed to be engaged. You should be showering me with flowers!'

'You've already had a very expensive ring,' he pointed out in a dour voice, knowing that he might as well have spared his breath. Polly was already bending over a bucket of mimosa.

'Shall we get some of this too?'

'Oh, yes, let's,' said Simon sarcastically. 'We've only got a garden full of the stuff at home!'

'I know, but it's such a shame to cut it and these are so gorgeous.' Blithely, she helped herself to two enormous bunches. 'And can we have some marguerites, as well?'

'Why don't you just buy the whole stall while you're at it?' said Simon, but he let her carry on picking out flowers until her arms were full.

'Oh, they're lovely!' she said, burying her face in the mass of blooms and breathing in their heady scent before looking up at Simon. 'I'll put my forty-eight francs towards them, if you like.'

Only Polly would offer to spend the only money she had on a bunch of flowers! 'That won't be necessary,' said Simon dryly. 'I'll buy you the flowers if you like them so much.'

'I do.' She rewarded him with a dazzling smile that almost stopped the breath in his throat.

Making himself turn to the delighted flower-seller, Simon asked how much he owed. Polly watched a little guiltily as he handed over what seemed like a huge handful of notes, and accepted a tiny amount of change from the flower-seller, who said something too quickly for Polly's limited French to understand.

'What did he say?' she asked Simon curiously as they walked across the square towards the car.

'He said you were beautiful,' he said after a tiny moment.

'Oh, how sweet of him!' Polly was thrilled. 'What did you say back to him?' She laughed, expecting Simon to have made some crushing comment about how much of a mess she always looked.

But instead he hesitated. He looked down at Polly, smiling in the sunlight, with her arms full of flowers, her face vivid and her eyes reflecting the blue of the Provence sky.

'I said that you were,' he admitted.

'Really?' Suspecting sarcasm, Polly glanced at him suspiciously, but he avoided her gaze.

'Come on, Polly,' he said gruffly, 'you must know that you're pretty.'

'I didn't know that you thought so,' she said. Her steps slowed, and she stopped, looking up at him almost uncertainly. 'Do you?'

Simon stopped too, and turned back to face her. They stood in the middle of the square and looked at each other, and it was as if they were enveloped in an airless bubble of silence, cutting them off from the parping car horns and chattering crowds and the hustle and bustle of the market.

Afterwards, Simon was never quite sure what he had been going to say. He did open his mouth to reply, but before he could say anything another voice broke through the invisible barrier that surrounded them.

'Polly?'

It took Polly a little while to realise that she was being addressed, and another, when she turned, to register that Philippe Ladurie was standing right in front of her.

She looked blankly at him for a moment before snapping abruptly to attention. 'Ph-Philippe!' she stammered, gathering herself together with an effort. 'I...I wasn't expecting to see you.'

That was good, thought Simon, observing her sourly. She had only dressed specially and spent the entire lunch scanning the crowds in the hope that she *would* see him!

'I thought it was you.' Philippe was charm itself. Careful not to crush the flowers in her arms, he kissed Polly four times, twice on either cheek. 'It's wonderful to see you again, Polly.'

'It's good to see you, too.' Polly was very conscious of Simon standing beside her, looking boot-faced. She felt a little odd. Surely she should be over the moon to see Philippe again, not wondering what Simon had been going to say, or what that strange look in his eyes had meant?

'Um...this is Simon Taverner,' she said, remembering her manners at last. 'Simon, this is Philippe Ladurie.'

'We've never met before,' said Philippe as the two

men exchanged a cool handshake, 'but of course I have heard a lot about you.'

'I've heard a lot about you, too,' said Simon with a glance at Polly.

'I was sorry I didn't get a chance to say goodbye to you, Philippe,' she said hurriedly. 'I'm afraid I left...unexpectedly.'

'So I heard.' Philippe laughed. 'I don't blame you at all for walking out. My sister can be a very difficult woman, especially to work for.'

'I didn't walk out,' said Polly, 'I was sacked.'

'Oh?' Philippe looked from her to Simon. 'Then it's not true that you're engaged?'

'Of course it's true,' said Simon in a flinty voice before Polly had a chance to answer. He put a possessive arm around Polly and pulled her against him. 'Why shouldn't it be?'

'We were just surprised that it was such a secret,' said Philippe, not unreasonably. He smiled at Polly. 'Congratulations!' he said, and glanced again at Simon. 'You are a lucky man!'

'Aren't I?' said Simon coldly.

Philippe was unfazed by his hostility. 'Are you staying near here?'

'Near Vesilloux,' said Polly, knowing that Simon would be as uninformative as possible. She tried to pull herself away from him surreptitiously but the arm around her was like steel. 'Do you know it?'

'Of course. We are practically neighbours! I live only at St Georges—it's very close to you.'

'Ten miles at least,' said Simon deflatingly, breaking in on this exchange. 'And on the other side of Marsillac. I'd hardly call us neighbours.'

'Let us say neighbours in spirit, then.' Philippe smiled charmingly.

There was a slight pause. Polly sought desperately for something to say, but there was a limit with Simon holding her clamped against him and deliberately cramping her style.

In the end, it was Philippe who broke it. 'So, Polly, you are going to marry an Englishman? Does that mean you're not interested in learning French any more?'

'No.' Polly trod firmly on Simon's foot, but, although he winced, he didn't relax his hold. 'No, I'm still keen. In fact,' she went on, more to annoy Simon than anything else, 'I was going to ring you. Simon's going back to work in a couple of weeks, and I thought I'd stay around for a while and really work on my French. I thought you might be able to recommend someone to give me lessons.'

'I'm sure there are teachers around, but the best way is just to speak French the whole time, and you don't need a teacher for that. I'd be delighted to give you some conversation lessons, Polly.'

'You don't mind, do you, darling?' she asked Simon provocatively, delighted to see that a muscle was twitching in his jaw. Serve him right for spoiling her meeting with Philippe. She hadn't been able to concentrate at all with his arm around her, holding her against the distracting hardness of his body.

'Of course not,' he said through gritted teeth.

'You must both come over before then,' said Philippe smoothly, and, seeing that Simon was about to refuse, Polly got in quickly.

'We'd love to,' she said and smiled brightly at Simon. 'Wouldn't we?'

Simon glared back at her. 'You know we've got visitors coming, sweetheart.'

'Bring them too,' said Philippe with easy charm. 'In fact, I'm having a party the weekend after next. Why don't you all come to that, and then we can fix up a date to start your French lessons?'

His eyes twinkled down at Polly, his smile so wickedly attractive that she couldn't help smiling back, although she was in truth rather overwhelmed by his assurance. She had been so used to adoring him from a distance that it was a little unsettling to find all her fantasies about meeting him again coming true.

'I'll look forward to it,' she managed to say coolly enough in the end.

Under Simon's glacial grey gaze, Philippe went though the whole business of kissing Polly lingeringly on the cheeks again. '*Au revoir*, Polly,' he murmured.

She swallowed. '*Au revoir.*'

'Goodbye,' said Simon very distinctly. He let Polly go at last, but only to take her arm in a firm grasp. 'Come along, *darling*,' he said. 'It's high time I took you home.'

CHAPTER SEVEN

'*AU REVOIR*,' Simon mimicked savagely as he frog-marched her away from Philippe.

Polly wrenched her arm out of his. 'If you didn't like the conversation, you could have gone and bought a paper or made some kind of excuse to leave us alone,' she said furiously. 'We would have got on a lot better without you, that's for sure!'

'God knows what you would have got up to if I'd left you two alone together! My presence didn't seem to stop you offering yourself to him on a plate as it was.' He scowled as he remembered how she had smiled at Philippe. 'French lessons! Hah! It's easy to see what kind of lessons *he's* got in mind!'

Polly's cheeks were flushed, her eyes stormy. 'Philippe's going to help me with my conversation, that's all.'

'A man like that has only got one kind of conversation. All you'll get is pillow talk!'

'Well, they say that's the best way to learn,' she said, goaded.

Simon opened the boot of the car so that she could lay the flowers in the dark and slammed it shut with unnecessary force. 'I wouldn't trust that man further than I could throw him!'

'Nobody's asking you to trust him.' Polly marched round to the passenger side and waited, fuming, while he unlocked the car. 'There was no need for you to be so rude to Philippe. I wouldn't have blamed him if he'd turned on his heel and left, but instead he had the courtesy to invite you to his party.'

'You don't think I want to go to any party of his, do you?' said Simon, banging his door and jabbing the key at the ignition as she got in beside him.

'Don't go,' she said promptly. 'I'd much rather go on my own anyway. I don't want you there cramping my style like you did today! You saw how interested Philippe was?'

Simon shoved the gearstick into reverse. 'Only because he thinks you're unavailable,' he said with a cynical look. 'He's that kind of man. He's only showing an interest now because I'm on the scene. He's the type who thinks a bit of competition spices things up, but as soon as he's broken up a perfectly good relationship he'll be bored and move on to some other woman who's offended his vanity by showing some interest in another man.'

'I don't know how you can tell all that when all you've done is shake hands with him,' snapped Polly, dismissing the uncomfortable idea that Philippe had indeed only approached her when he'd seen her watching Simon at the party. 'He's a very nice man,' she said defiantly.

Simon snorted. 'What on earth do you see in him?'

'Charm,' she said. 'Wit, good looks, intelligence, sincerity...none of which *you* would know anything about, of course!'

'Charm? All he can do is smile!'

'It's much more than that,' Polly insisted. 'Philippe's glamorous and exciting. He makes life *fun*. You and Helena might like to spend your day writing out lists and organising every five minutes, but I want to have a good time. Philippe's got a yacht. He races speed-

boats. He skis and he climbs and he goes to casinos
and smart parties.'

'In other words, he does absolutely nothing produc-
tive or useful.'

'You know your trouble?' said Polly, tossing back
her hair. 'You're jealous!'

'Jealous?' Simon achieved an incredulous laugh.
'Philippe Ladurie doesn't have a single thing that I
want!'

Nothing at all? He changed gear with controlled fury
as the image of Polly's face lifted so adoringly to the
Frenchman's swam into his mind. Philippe was welcome to her! Let him cope with her mess and her
snippy comments and her complete lack of responsibility.

And with her smile and her kisses and the way she
turned her face up to the sun?

Simon pushed the image firmly aside. Let Philippe
cope with all of it. There was nothing of his that Simon
wanted. Nothing at all.

They drove back to La Treille and unloaded the car
in tight-lipped silence.

'I'm having a swim,' Polly announced as soon as
she had put the flowers to soak in a large bucket.

'Oh, no, you don't!' said Simon. 'We're going to
put all this lot away first.'

'Can't it wait?'

'No, it can't. It's been sitting in a hot car for a good
two hours.'

Polly sighed and began unpacking bags with bad
grace, but whenever she tried to put anything in a cupboard Simon would snatch it out of her hand and put
it somewhere else with a lecture on kitchen organisation.

'It's known as logic,' he said. 'Have you ever heard of that, Polly?'

Polly had had enough. She was hot, tired and cross. 'Have you ever heard of a punch on the nose?' she retorted, throwing a packet of sugar onto the table. 'You put it all away if it matters so much! I'm going for a swim!'

He was impossible! Polly swam furiously up and down the pool. Nit-picking, domineering, superior…he was *worse* now than he had been as a boy! She would be lucky if he hadn't spoilt her chances with Philippe for good. If she had had any sense, she would have gone off with Philippe there and then and left Simon to his lists and perfectly organised kitchen!

It took several laps before the quietness and the cool, clear water began to calm her temper. Turning on her back, Polly floated for a while and mused as she looked up at the sky. If only Simon didn't make her feel so edgy. She never seemed to know where she was with him now. She would be enjoying his company one minute, only to find herself longing to hit him the next. When he wasn't being utterly infuriating, he could be really quite nice. Last night, for instance, they had got on well, and things hadn't been going that badly today until Philippe had turned up.

Polly closed her eyes against the sun and saw Simon's face as he'd pushed the ring onto her finger that morning in the jeweller's, and her hand tingled in the water as if the brush of his fingers were burnt onto her skin. Then for some reason she found herself thinking about his expression when they had stopped in the street and she had asked him if he really did think that she was pretty. What had he been about to say?

A tiny frown creased Polly's forehead. She should be dreaming about Philippe, not Simon. Where *was* Simon, anyway? She opened her eyes with a tiny sigh. He was probably still colour-coding the shopping, or filing fruit in alphabetical order. Polly didn't know what a glamorous girl like Helena saw in him. He was so uptight about everything!

There was nothing uptight about the way he kissed, though...

Polly rolled abruptly back onto her front and began swimming again. Damn! What had made her think about kissing him when she had done such a good job of putting it out of her mind today? Now that the memory was back, it was stuck right where she wouldn't be able to forget the feel of his lips or the touch of his hand against her skin or the terrifying sense that the flicker of excitement might burst at any moment into an uncontrollable flame, and *then* where would they be?

Taking a deep breath, Polly dived determinedly under the water as if she could simply rinse those disturbing memories away, but when she burst up to the surface again, shaking the water from her eyes and smoothing the wet hair back from her face with both hands, the first thing she saw was Simon and the world rocked alarmingly around her.

There was nothing surprising about seeing him there—it was his pool, after all—but Polly felt as if the air had been driven from her lungs in a sickening blow. He was standing by the edge of the pool, holding a glass of wine in each hand, and as she looked up at him he seemed to be silhouetted against the sky by the dazzling Mediterranean light.

'I've brought you a peace-offering,' he said, lifting a glass.

'Oh.' Telling herself that her breathlessness was only a result of her dive, Polly swam over and climbed up the steps by his feet. She felt jolted, jarred, rattled by the way all her senses had jumped to attention at the mere sight of him.

Squeezing the worst of the water from her hair with one hand, she accepted a glass from Simon with the other. Was it her imagination, or was he careful to make sure that their fingers didn't touch? 'Thanks,' she said a little shyly. 'I don't think I've done anything to deserve it, though.'

'I think I owe you an apology.' Simon cleared his throat. He wished Polly would cover herself up. The sight of her standing in a bikini with the water dripping off her lush golden skin was proving uncomfortably distracting. 'I've been on edge about this new merger and making sure the meeting with Julien goes well, and I'm afraid I took it out on you,' he said gruffly, managing to wrench his eyes away at last.

'That's all right,' said Polly awkwardly, rather thrown. She was used to Simon being cutting or exasperated or mocking. An apologetic Simon was something new and she wasn't sure how to deal with it at all! 'I don't suppose I'm that easy to be with, either,' she offered.

Simon allowed himself to glance at her. The wet bikini was doing all that it was designed to do, showing off her long legs and clinging to her generous curves, but right then he wished it would transform itself into a voluminous caftan. 'No,' he agreed wryly.

His gaze had barely glanced over her, but Polly was suddenly conscious that she was almost naked, and she put down her glass so that she could wrap a towel protectively around her. 'Sorry,' she said without really knowing what she was apologising for.

'It's not your fault.' Simon's smile was twisted. He sat down on the edge of one of the poolside loungers and rested his arms on his knees, twisting his glass absently between his hands as if trying to make up his mind about something. 'Are you sure you want to go on with this, Polly?' he asked abruptly at last.

'What do you mean?' Polly's towel slipped as she sank down onto a lounger facing him, and she grabbed at it, tucking it securely around her chest.

'I've been thinking.' Simon looked down into his wine. After Polly had stormed out, he had finished putting everything away in a cold fury, but when he had finished he had looked round at the immaculate kitchen and realised that it looked somehow empty. Its clean lines and gleaming functionality had always pleased his eye before; now they seemed cold and cheerless.

Love is about a room that feels empty when the person you love isn't in it. Polly's voice had echoed in Simon's head as he'd stood in the middle of the still kitchen, remembering the blueness of her eyes and the warmth of her smile and the way her hair had fallen over her cheek as she had buried her face in the flowers.

He'd frowned. He couldn't be in love with Polly. He *wasn't* in love with her.

But perhaps he hadn't been entirely fair to her either.

Simon had stood thinking for some time, then he'd poured wine into two glasses and deliberately left the cork lying on the table. It might not be much of a mess, but it was a gesture in the right direction.

'Your parents have done a lot for me, Polly,' he said

now, lifting his eyes to her face. 'It was your father who supported me through university and gave me advice and encouragement when I first set up on my own. I didn't repay them well by demanding that you act as my fiancée in return for a lift in the car.'

Simon's expression was grim. 'I should never ever have thought of it. What I *should* have done was insist on lending you enough money to live comfortably until you decided what you wanted to do—and that's what I want to do now. We can go to the bank tomorrow and I'll get you some cash, and you can go before Chantal and Julien arrive. You don't have to pretend to be my fiancée any more.'

Polly stared at him in bewilderment. 'But...what about Julien and the merger? I thought it was really important to you?'

'It is,' said Simon. 'And not just for me. It's just as important for all the people who work for me. Together we've been trying to break into Europe for some time, and this is our best chance yet. Julien has seen our proposals, and it's those that will win us the contract in the end, but I don't want to alienate him on a personal level or that could spoil everything that we've all worked so hard for. That's why I needed you.'

There was a dull feeling in Polly's chest. 'Are you trying to say that you don't need me any more?'

Simon looked across at her. Her eyes were very blue between wet, spiky lashes and they held an oddly hurt expression. Droplets of water still glistened on the smooth, golden shoulders, and trickled slowly down into the tantalising glimpse of cleavage beneath the towel. Simon averted his eyes and frowned down into his glass. The last thing he wanted right now was to start noticing the generous curve of her mouth or the warm, inviting texture of her skin.

'It's not that I don't need you,' he said. 'I do. But it's not fair to keep you here just because of some silly deal we made if you would really rather be with Philippe. I know I'm boring compared to him,' he went on heroically, 'and it hasn't exactly been fun for you so far with me biting your head off or ordering you around. You can take the money tomorrow and go and have a good time with him instead. I know that's what you want.'

He paused. 'Just be careful you don't get hurt, though,' he muttered.

'I'm not taking any money.' Polly found her voice at last. Simon had just offered her the perfect get-out, and she was disconcerted to discover that she didn't want it.

'I don't have much pride,' she told him, moving over to sit next to him on the lounger, 'but even I wouldn't accept money from you just to have a holiday. I know that you probably only offered to pay me to be your fiancée as a way of giving me money without hurting my feelings, and the least I can do is earn it. You know it's a point of principle with me to always fulfil my contract! If you want me to go, you're going to have to sack me like Martine Sterne.

'Besides, I'm enjoying it,' she went on with a smile. 'Where else could I find a job where I got taken out to lunch and dinner, and had flowers bought for me, and could spend all afternoon lolling by a pool like this?'

'At Philippe's house,' Simon forced himself to point out.

'I don't know that,' she said quickly. 'You're the one who said I don't know him very well.'

Polly was surprised at how desperate she was to convince Simon to let her stay. 'I know I've spent most of the day grumbling, but I'm really not in any hurry to go. As far as I'm concerned, it's a perfect situation,' she told him. 'I get to stay in a beautiful place and have a good time for two weeks, and at the end I'll have enough money to be independent.

'It would be fun to see Philippe after that,' she went on, unsure whether she was trying to reassure Simon or herself, 'but two weeks isn't going to make much difference, and if nothing comes of it I'll be able to move on feeling that I've earned my money. If I just take it from you as a loan, I'll have to do something sensible with it, and I don't want that!'

Simon smiled at that. 'I just don't want you to feel that acting as my fiancée is going to put you in an awkward situation,' he said, choosing his words carefully.

'It won't,' said Polly. 'I mean, it's true that it *has* been a little awkward,' she said. 'Some parts weren't quite as easy as I thought they would be.' She hesitated, glancing at Simon under her lashes. 'I was really nervous about sleeping with you last night,' she confessed in a rush.

Simon's mouth twisted ruefully. 'So was I.'

'Really?'

'Really.'

Polly suddenly felt a whole lot better. 'It's silly, isn't it?' she said, taking his hand. 'We're friends. Pretending to be engaged to each other oughtn't to be a big deal. We should just relax and enjoy it. It could be fun!'

Simon thought about sharing a bed with Polly for the next two weeks without touching her and wasn't sure that 'fun' was exactly the right word.

Seeing the doubt in his face, Polly wondered in sudden dismay if he was thinking of Helena. It must be hard for him having her here when all he really wanted was Helena, and what if he thought he was being somehow disloyal?

'We wouldn't hurt anybody by pretending,' she said persuasively. 'It's not as if we'd be having a real relationship.'

'No,' Simon agreed. He turned his head and his eyes met Polly's warm blue ones. 'It's not as if it's real,' he echoed slowly.

'And it would be silly to waste this ring after we spent all that time choosing it,' she pointed out, displaying her left hand with its glinting jewels. 'I'm just getting used to it!'

Simon smiled, but his voice was serious as he asked: 'Are you sure, Polly? I don't want to take advantage of you, that's all.'

'I'm quite sure.' Polly was conscious of a disproportionate sense of relief that she was going to be allowed to stay instead of being free to go wherever she wanted and do whatever she wanted with money in her pocket and no strings attached.

Simon suddenly realised that he was holding her hand a little too tightly and let it go. 'If you really are prepared to stay, I'd be very grateful. It means a lot to me.'

'Good. That's settled, then.' Polly's hand felt lost without his warm clasp. 'I'm sorry I was so horrible earlier on,' she said almost shyly. 'I really am going to try and be a bit tidier.'

'If you do, I'll try and be more relaxed,' Simon promised. 'I suppose I am a bit obsessive about organisation. It think it comes from being the eldest in a family that's so laid-back that nothing would ever get done unless I did it. You know what Mother's like, and Emily and Charlie are as bad.'

It was true, Polly thought, contrite. She had always adored Simon's mother, whose chaotic approach to life was so like her own, but there was no denying that she was utterly dependent on Simon to sort out her affairs for her.

Sitting by the pool in the bright light of Provence, Polly wondered for the first time what it had been like for Simon when his father had died, leaving him responsible for his lovable but scatty family. He had only been fourteen, just a boy, and she had been only seven at the time, too young to appreciate that perhaps Simon had had little choice but to be the organised member of the family.

With an inward grimace, she remembered how she and Charlie and Emily had moaned about Simon's bossiness and taunted him with his attempts to instil some order into the chaos of the family home. Her parents had been the only ones who had offered the young Simon any support at all, and he had never forgotten it.

'The next time we go shopping,' she said, 'I promise I'll make a list.'

Simon laughed. 'It's a deal.'

There was a pause. This was the moment for her to get up and move back to her own lounger, Polly realised, but she didn't move. She could hear the cicadas shrilling frantically in the grass behind her, could feel the dampness of her bikini against her flesh and the softness of the towel over her thighs.

Simon reached out and tucked a lock of wet hair behind her ear. 'Do you think this would be a good time for our daily kiss?' he asked slowly.

'Why not?' said Polly before she had a chance to lose her nerve. This was her idea, after all, and the sooner she started to think of it as a daily exercise, the better! It didn't stop a peculiar mixture of anticipation and fright fluttering underneath her skin as they shifted to face each other.

'OK,' said Simon, hoping that he sounded suitably brisk and cheerful. It was all very well for Polly to talk about getting used to kissing each other, but it was rather different when you had to put it into practice!

Leaning forward awkwardly, he bumped noses with Polly who had leant at the same time, and they both found a release for their nerves in laughter. 'You were right,' he said. 'We definitely need practice!'

'It was easier yesterday when we weren't trying,' she said unthinkingly, and then wished she hadn't. It reminded her too vividly of how nice that kiss had been. She wasn't supposed to enjoy this. She was supposed to be thinking of kissing Simon as a casual thing, something she took for granted, a part of the daily routine, like washing up or doing her teeth.

'Let's have another go.' Simon leant forward again, more carefully this time, and Polly leant too, and their mouths found each other naturally after all. They kissed softly, once, twice, a third time before drawing apart very slightly to look into each other's eyes.

For a moment they hesitated. It would have been easy to have sat back and ended it there, but something stronger seemed to be pulling them together, a deep, magnetic attraction that neither could resist. Polly's lips parted instinctively as Simon's mouth found hers, and they kissed once more, a deep, dangerously sweet kiss that began softly but grew in urgency with terrifying speed.

Polly put her hands to Simon's shoulders for support as she felt herself tugged by a powerful undertow of excitement. It wasn't supposed to feel this good, she thought hazily. It wasn't supposed to feel this *right*. They should stop...but how could she stop when her blood was pounding and every sense was urging her to lean closer?

And then Simon took the decision away from her by putting his arms around her almost roughly and pulling her hard against him and Polly gave up any attempt to think. Winding her arms round his neck, she abandoned herself joyously to the sheer pleasure surging through her. How could she think when Simon's warm hand had pushed aside the towel and was smoothing possessively over her back, making her shiver as it curved around her side, and slid insistently down over the damp bikini at her hip and along her thigh?

It was left to Simon to keep a last tenuous grip on reality and realise that things were rapidly escalating out of control. Very reluctantly, he forced himself to lift his head and draw back, but his hand seemed to be suckered onto her soft skin and it took a huge effort to lift it away.

Polly only just stopped herself murmuring in protest. Her arms fell from his neck and she sat giddily back, swallowing hard to disguise the frantic trembling inside her. 'I...I think we're getting better, don't you?' she made herself say, although all the breath seemed to have been sucked from her body and her voice came out high and uneven.

Simon forced a smile. He was having trouble with his own breathing. 'We need to work on the opening sequence, but otherwise there doesn't seem to be a problem,' he agreed.

'No.' Polly's bones felt as if they had liquefied, but somehow she managed to retrieve her towel and get herself back onto the opposite lounger. She was terrified that if she stayed so close she would do something she regretted. Her body was acting so strangely that she couldn't trust it not to clamp itself back against Simon's.

Instead, she made herself reach down for the wineglass she had set on the stones an aeon ago, but her hand was shaking so much that the glass knocked against her teeth and she had to put it down again. 'Well,' she said rather hopelessly.

Simon ran his hands threw his hair and took a steadying breath. 'Well,' he agreed. There didn't seem to be much else to say.

His body was pounding, his senses reeling, and it was all he could do not to jerk Polly to her feet and drag her up to his bedroom where he could peel off that damp bikini and make long, sweet love to her. Simon looked down at his palms which were still pulsing with the feel of her and knew with a sickening sense of inevitability that he wanted her with an intensity that he had never experienced before.

God, what was he *thinking* of? This was Polly, Polly whom he remembered with pigtails, scabbed knees and a gap between her teeth. The same Polly who had whispered behind her hand with his sister and collapsed so irritatingly into giggles at the slightest opportunity.

Polly who had slavishly followed fashion, who had teetered around on unsuitable shoes and done extraordinary things to her hair, who had tried her best to rebel against her loving parents without ever quite being able to achieve it.

Who had grown unexpectedly into a beautiful, desirable woman.

Simon took a fortifying slug of wine. He couldn't even think about it. She was still John's daughter, she was still Emily's best friend. The Armstrongs were family. Polly wasn't someone he could have an affair with and then go separate ways when it was over. She would be there at every family party, at every wedding, at every christening. The potential for tension, for hurt and embarrassment, was enormous.

Quite apart from anything else, Simon reminded himself, there was no reason to think that Polly wanted anything more from him than an undemanding two weeks. She might kiss him as if she were on fire, but Polly had always thrown herself into whatever she was doing. It didn't matter whether it was roller-skating or cooking or kissing, Polly would be doing it wholeheartedly.

The daily kiss so that they could get used to each other was one of her typically impulsive ideas, Simon thought wryly. She probably even believed that it would work! For her, he was a familiar figure, someone it was a little awkward to kiss, but certainly not anyone whose kisses could be taken seriously. Simon looked morosely down into his glass. He suspected that, for Polly, kissing him was something between a chore and a challenge, hardly more than a way of passing the time until she could go and throw herself at her precious

Frenchman who might amuse himself with her for a while before he hurt her.

Under her lashes, Polly saw him scowl and bit her lip. He looked so grim that she wondered if he was thinking about Helena. It would be awful if Simon was feeling guilty or uncomfortable about a kiss that she had practically forced on him! It had seemed such a good idea at the time, but she knew how dangerously close they had come to losing control. If Simon hadn't stopped when he did, she would have been ripping off his shirt and begging him to make love to her.

But he had stopped. Polly told herself that she was glad. Their kisses might not mean anything, but, if she were Helena, she didn't think she would like the idea of Simon kissing another girl, even if it *was* just John Armstrong's silly daughter.

Twisting the sapphire and diamond ring around her finger, Polly debated whether to suggest that it would be better if they didn't kiss again. But if she did that Simon would think that she had taken the whole thing seriously. What if he was afraid that she was going to do something stupid, like fall in love with him? Polly cringed at the thought. The whole idea was ridiculous, of course—wasn't she just *longing* for the chance to fall in love with Philippe?—but if it even crossed his mind it would make things excruciatingly embarrassing.

No, somehow she had to make it clear that she stood in no danger of doing anything of the kind. She needed to let Simon know that she wasn't going to take any of his kisses at all seriously, that she had no intention of getting involved, and that she wasn't about to forget that he had a perfectly good girlfriend to kiss whenever he wanted to!

In the lengthening silence, Polly cast around desperately for something to say to show how cool and unconcerned she was by the whole incident.

'Um…have you told Helena yet that I'm standing in for her?' she asked at last. It didn't come out quite as coolly as she had intended, but it was the best she could do.

Simon looked up, and the keenness of his grey eyes made Polly's heart bump against her ribs. 'No,' he said. 'Not yet.'

How could he explain to Polly why he hadn't rung his girlfriend without letting on that Helena wasn't his girlfriend at all? It would spoil everything if she knew. Every time he kissed her, every time he touched her, she would be wondering if he was taking it all a bit too seriously.

'I don't want to distract her,' he said after a moment. 'She's working on a difficult case and she's going to be preoccupied with that for the next couple of weeks at least. I'll tell her when it's over.'

'Maybe she'll have time to come down and join you for the rest of your holiday.'

'Maybe,' said Simon in a noncommittal voice. 'We'll have to see what happens.' He mustered a smile. 'You won't be around, anyway. You'll be off having a good time with Philippe by then.'

'Yes,' said Polly unenthusiastically. If everything worked out, Helena and Simon would have the holiday they deserved and she would get together with Philippe and have a wonderful, exciting time going to casinos and sitting on yachts. It would all be perfect. It should have sounded exactly what she wanted.

But somehow it didn't.

CHAPTER EIGHT

SOMETHING had changed down by the pool. Polly lay in the dark next to Simon that night, and listened to his slow, steady breathing. Things should have been easier now that they had cleared the air, but if anything they were more difficult.

The snappy, irritable edge to their exchanges had gone, it was true, but only to be replaced by another, much more disturbing kind of tension—the kind that made perfectly ordinary conversations fizzle out in mid-sentence and silences stretch until her nerves twanged and she rushed back into speech.

The kind that made her excruciatingly aware of the line of Simon's mouth and the deftness of his long, capable fingers and the hard solidity of his body lying only inches away.

What was wrong with her? Polly wondered with frustration. After a rocky start, this was shaping up to be one of the best summers of her life. There was no way she could earn so much money with so little effort anywhere else. Philippe had been more than friendly. His words might be innocuous enough, but those brown eyes had held more than a hint of promise. She ought to be over the moon at the idea that she might have caught the attention of a man more handsome and glamorous than her wildest dreams. Why wasn't she thinking about *him*?

Why was she thinking instead of Simon and the feel of his lips on hers? Turning restlessly on her side, Polly looked at the diffused moonlight curving over his shoulder and imagined reaching out to run her hand down his bare arm. How could Helena bear to work when she could be down here with the cicadas outside the window and the scented air, with the pool and the cool, quiet house and long nights alone with Simon?

She must be very sure of him. Polly rolled over to face the window with a sigh. Why shouldn't she be? Helena was everything Simon had said: attractive, intelligent, glamorous. The perfect partner for him in every way.

'What time are Chantal and Julien arriving?'

Polly was arranging the flowers in two huge vases. For some reason she hadn't slept well and she had woken feeling vaguely depressed. She was determined to make an effort to earn the money Simon was paying her, though, telling herself that if she could treat it as just another job she might feel less awkward about being with Simon.

'Chantal said they would try to get here by six,' said Simon, finishing his coffee. The kitchen might not be as tidy as he would like it, but it was strangely restful to sit at the table and watch Polly lift one stem at a time and place it carefully in the vase, her face intent as she stood back to judge the effect. 'We've got plenty of time to get ready for them.'

'I thought I'd cook them a nice meal tonight.' She glanced at him, pushing her hair over her shoulder. 'Don't worry, I won't destroy the kitchen!'

'Do you need a hand?'

'No.' Why did she suddenly feel so shy with him? It was *stupid*, Polly scolded herself, but she couldn't stop her eyes sliding away from his. 'I'll be fine.'

'Great.'

There was a pause. Polly concentrated on her flowers. Simon put his cup down in his saucer and looked out of the window, conscious of a tension seeping back into the atmosphere.

'Well, if there's nothing I can do...' He got to his feet, hating the forced heartiness in his voice.

Polly swallowed. Now was her chance to prove that, as far as she was concerned, this was just a job. She wasn't sure whether she needed to prove it to Simon or to herself, but she was hoping that if she could the tension simmering in the air would dissolve.

'There is one thing,' she said, putting down her secateurs. 'I need to kiss you.'

Simon froze in the act of picking up his cup and saucer. He looked at Polly, grey eyes alert and wary. It had taken him all night to talk himself into thinking of her as 'just Polly' again, and a kiss like the one by the pool would just put him back to square one. 'Now?' he said cautiously.

Polly didn't want to tell him that she wanted to get it over with so that she didn't have to spend the whole day praying that she wouldn't lose her self-control the way she had done yesterday afternoon.

'We might as well. It's not supposed to be romantic. It's supposed to be something we do as a matter of course.'

'OK.' Hoping that it didn't look too obvious that he was bracing himself, Simon went round the table to meet her.

Polly put her palms flat against his chest and looked into his face. She had planned to kiss him properly, but at the last moment her courage deserted her and she touched her lips to the corner of his mouth instead.

Simon deliberately kept his arms by his sides as she kissed him, but as she drew back he lifted his hands again to place them gently against her cheeks. 'Very good,' he said, cradling her face between his palms. 'It's my go now.' And, telling himself that he was just doing it to prove that he didn't have to lose control whenever he touched her, he bent his head and kissed her full on the mouth.

This time Polly was better prepared for the dizzying rush of pleasure. True, her fingers curled against the soft cotton of his shirt, but she didn't feel as if the ground had dropped away beneath her feet the way she had before, and she had hardly begun to congratulate herself on not overreacting than the kiss was over. Simon's hands fell from her face and they looked at each other with barely disguised relief.

'I think you were right,' he said slowly. 'Practice does make perfect. We're getting quite good at this!'

'I told you we would.' Polly checked cautiously for awkwardness in the atmosphere, but there didn't seem to be any at all. It had been a nice kiss—a *very* nice kiss, in fact—but she hadn't dissolved into a gibbering wreck the way she had whenever Simon had touched her before, and the air wasn't jangling with tension the way it had before.

Maybe this would work after all! Her spirits soared. If they could avoid any repetition of the agonising tension that had left her so crippled with shyness last night and this morning, they could really enjoy the next couple of weeks. And once Chantal and Julien were here, things could only get easier.

Her bizarre response to Simon's previous kisses must have been no more than reaction to tiredness or nerves, Polly decided confidently. Obviously she had been making a fuss about nothing. Now they could just get back to their old relationship, and everything would be fine.

'What lovely flowers!' Chantal admired the vase that Polly had stood on the hearth, the bright colours a vivid contrast to the grey stone.

Some of Polly's confidence had deserted her when she'd first laid eyes on Chantal. Simon's ex-girlfriend was dark and petite, with long, green eyes, depressingly flawless skin and the kind of bone structure Polly could only dream about. She wore loose fawn trousers and a little white shirt with perfectly knotted scarf. Next to her, Polly felt scruffy and fat.

She warmed slightly to her as Chantal exclaimed over the flowers. Simon had made a heroic effort and refrained from comment, but Polly knew that he hated the way the flowers were jumbled haphazardly together. He would no doubt have preferred some striking, minimalist arrangement, and it was some comfort to know that Chantal at least liked the effect.

'It's not at all like your flat in London, Simon,' said Chantal, looking around her with pleasure.

It wasn't now, thought Simon wryly. Polly had done her best to tidy, but she seemed unaware of the fact that in two short days her belongings had migrated over the house and made themselves at home among his furniture. The glass coffee-table, normally starkly bare and effective, was now cluttered with books, magazines, a couple of dirty mugs and a half-empty glass, emery boards, nail varnish and the postcards that she had started to write but hadn't finished.

'Polly's responsible for the change in atmosphere,' he said dryly.

Chantal smiled at Polly. 'I used to try and make Simon's flat more feminine, but he would never let me alter anything,' she said. 'You must be very special!'

'She is.'

Simon put his arm around Polly, who made herself relax against him. She had seen Julien frown, too.

He was some years older than Chantal, and very attractive in a passionate, brooding sort of way. He obviously adored his wife, and could hardly take his eyes off her. It was equally obvious that he hadn't liked her casual reference to the time when she had been part of Simon's life.

Polly wouldn't have liked it either if she had been him, especially given the warmth of the hug Simon had given Chantal when they'd arrived. She had observed it as balefully as Julien, and couldn't help reflecting that Helena might be a little less sure of Simon if she saw the way he welcomed his ex-girlfriend. Simon had certainly never kissed *her* with that kind of affection, Polly thought.

'I'm so pleased to meet you at last,' Chantal was saying to her. 'You're not at all as I expected!'

'Oh? Why not?' asked Polly, although she thought she probably knew.

'It's hard to say… I suppose you look so much more relaxed than Simon made you sound. And you look very young to be a successful lawyer,' Chantal added tactfully, obviously afraid that her first comment might not sound very flattering.

'I think you're muddling Polly up with Helena,' said Simon easily after only the tiniest of pauses. He had been hoping that Chantal wouldn't know very much about Helena, but obviously he had told her more than he had thought.

Embarrassed, Chantal clapped a hand to her mouth. 'Helena, of course! I'm so sorry, Polly! But I'm sure you didn't tell me, Simon,' she accused him. 'When did all this happen?'

'A couple of months ago. Things just fizzled out with Helena.' Simon lifted his hand to stroke a strand of golden hair tenderly behind Polly's ear. 'And then I met Polly again, and…boom!…that was it!'

Chantal laughed. 'I knew it would happen to you one day, Simon! You just had to wait for the right girl.'

'Yes,' he agreed slowly, looking down at Polly, whose face was burning where his fingers had brushed against her temple. His arm tightened around her. 'And now I know I've found her.'

Polly's heart squeezed at the look in Simon's eyes. It would be so easy to let herself believe that it were true. She had to remember that it was all an act, and it was time that she played her part.

'Shall we tell them?' she asked him, as if they hadn't rehearsed this very moment.

'Why not?' he said.

Polly turned to Chantal and Julien and smiled as she showed them the ring on her finger. 'Simon and I got engaged yesterday,' she told them.

Surely Chantal at least must be able to see it for the lie it was? She knew Simon, knew the kind of elegant, composed women that he liked, women like her. How could she possibly believe that he would fall in love with a scruffy girl who never had the discipline to stick to a diet for more than half a day and who disrupted his neat, ordered life with her awkwardness and her mess?

Polly waited for Chantal to laugh, or point an accusing finger, but she didn't even look surprised.

Instead, she seemed genuinely thrilled, hugging first Polly and then Simon. 'That's wonderful news!' she cried.

Julien's expression had lightened noticeably. 'Congratulations,' he said, wringing Simon's hand.

Watching his reaction, Simon told himself that the pretence was worth it. If Julien relaxed, they would be able to discuss the merger properly, and surely that was the most important thing? There had been times over the last couple of days when he had almost forgotten the merger, times like just now when he had looked down into Polly's blue eyes and realised how easy it would be to forget that he was pretending at all.

Julien's arrival had reminded him—not before time!—just what this was all about. All he had to do was keep telling himself how important the merger was to the company, and it would be easy to resist the distraction of Polly's eyes, and Polly's lips and the soft roundness of Polly's body pressed against his.

Easy.

Chantal and Julien insisted on opening a bottle of champagne. 'To Polly and Simon!' they said, lifting their glasses.

Polly smiled politely and glanced at Simon. It was obvious that some gesture was required.

Simon must have had the same thought, for he slid his hand beneath her hair to rest at the nape of her neck and tug her head gently towards him. Polly went unresisting, closing her eyes as he kissed her and allowing herself for a brief, treacherous moment to imagine what it would be like if it were for real.

She sat back as Simon released her, half relieved, half disappointed that the kiss had been so brief. It had felt quite natural, and, judging by Chantal and Julien's smiling expressions, it had looked natural, too.

'Tell us how you met,' said Chantal eagerly. 'I want to know all about it!'

They had known that the question was bound to come up, so had decided to stick to the truth as far as possible. 'We've known each other for ever,' said Polly. 'We spent all our holidays together as children, but once Simon left home we went our different ways. We'd hardly seen each other over the last few years until we met up again recently.'

Chantal was delighted. 'So you were childhood sweethearts?'

'Not exactly,' said Simon in a dry voice, taking Polly's hand. 'Although Polly was very keen to marry me when she was four.'

'To tell you the truth, we never got on at all,' said Polly quickly before he got started on *that* story. 'I thought Simon was incredibly boring and he thought I was incredibly silly!' She made herself look at Simon with a smile. 'You did, didn't you?'

'I've changed my mind,' he said, and the grey eyes looking directly back into hers held an expression that sent a blush stealing up Polly's cheeks.

Chantal laughed. 'So what made you change *your* mind, Polly?'

'I don't know,' said Polly slowly, very aware of Simon holding her hand in a warm, strong clasp. 'One minute Simon was just an irritating family friend and the next…' She trailed off, her expression puzzled, and Chantal finished her sentence for her.

'And the next you were in love with him?'

Polly's heart stumbled. She felt as if she had been brought up short on the very edge of a dizzying abyss,

knowing that one false step would send her tumbling
into the unknown. The feeling was so strong that she
could only stare wide-eyed back at Chantal while her
mind made her step very cautiously back from the
edge. Of course she wasn't in love with Simon! She
was just getting carried away by the pretence.

Wasn't she?

'Polly?' They were all looking at her curiously and
Polly pulled herself together with an effort.

'Yes,' she said, moistening her lips. 'That's how it
was.'

'Was it the same for you, Simon?' Chantal asked.

'I think I fell in love with her the moment I saw her
again,' he said, lifting Polly's hand and uncurling her
fingers so that he could press a warm kiss into her
palm. She drew a sharp breath as the feel of it shuddered up her arm and then snaked slowly, seductively,
down her spine.

'You're making that up!' she said unevenly, pretending to tease, but Simon met her mock accusing
gaze with disturbing steadiness.

'No, I'm not. When you opened that door you
looked so different from what I remembered. I felt as
if I'd never seen you before. I tried to go on thinking
of you as I'd thought of you before, but it wasn't any
good. By the time I'd realised what had happened, I
was hopelessly in love with you and it was too late to
do anything about it.'

His eyes were warmer than Polly had ever seen them
before. He's just pretending, she tried to remind herself, but as she looked almost helplessly back at him it
was as if the two of them were quite alone. She could
feel her pulse beating beneath her skin, and there was
a quivering deep inside her.

'You didn't tell me that before,' she managed, hanging onto the pretence with difficulty.

'I didn't want to until I was sure that you loved me too...but you do, don't you?'

'Yes,' said Polly. Afterwards she told herself that there was nothing else she could have said, but at the time the answer came unthinkingly to her lips. 'Yes, I do.'

And then, as if they had practised it, they leant into each other and exchanged a kiss so sweet that when they broke apart Polly realised to her horror that there were tears in her eyes.

Not that Chantal and Julien seemed to think that there was anything amiss. Both were beaming, and Julien lifted his glass in another toast. 'To love!' he said.

Polly's hand was shaking, but, conscious of Simon's eyes on her, she picked up her glass with a brave smile. 'To love!' she echoed and made herself look at him the way she would naturally do if they did love each other.

There was an odd expression in Simon's eyes as he looked back at her. He lifted his own glass to toast her in return. 'To love,' he said.

Simon had winced at the state of the kitchen when Polly had finished cooking, but he had to admit that out of the chaos she had produced a delicious meal, and by the time they had had the champagne and drunk the wine that Julien had produced they had both been able to relax and enjoy themselves far more than either of them had expected to at the beginning of the evening.

He was smiling as he closed the bedroom door that

night, and he turned to sweep Polly up in a big hug. 'We did it!' he said jubilantly.

Laughing, Polly hugged him back. 'Don't tell me Julien has agreed to the merger already!'

'Not yet, but we got on well and I know he's going to look at our proposal very seriously.' Still holding Polly, he smiled down into her face. 'Julien's obviously relaxed and is prepared to enjoy himself while he's here, and that's thanks to you, Polly. You were fantastic!'

Polly was very conscious of his hands, hard against her waist. 'You weren't so bad yourself,' she replied lightly, trying to ignore his closeness.

'Julien spent a lot of time telling me how lucky I am to have you,' Simon told her and she made herself smile back at him.

'Chantal's been telling me the same thing about you. They've got no idea that we're not really in love.'

'No,' he said slowly. 'We were pretty convincing, weren't we?'

'We must be natural actors,' Polly suggested, uncomfortably aware of the unevenness in her voice.

'We must be.' Unthinkingly, Simon tightened his hold, sliding his hands around her back, but the feel of the silky material of her dress slipping over her skin beneath his fingers brought him to his senses with something like a physical shock. He was abruptly aware of how close she was, of the warmth of her body and the scent of her perfume, of how easy—how dangerously easy—it would be to pull her closer, and his hands dropped as he stepped back almost brusquely.

There was an awkward pause. 'Well,' he said uncomfortably at last. 'We'd better go to bed. It's been a long day.'

'Yes.' Polly cleared her throat. 'I'll…er…I'll just go and do my teeth.'

She fled into the bathroom, aghast to discover when she began to take off her make-up that her hands were shaking. For one breathless moment then she had been so sure that Simon was about to pull her into his arms, and she had been shocked at the intensity of the disappointment that had speared her when he had put her firmly away from him instead.

She had been so good today, too. After that reassuringly controlled kiss this morning, Polly had convinced herself that she could relax and enjoy herself, and everything had been fine until Simon had hugged her just now.

It was all his fault, Polly told herself, wiping off mascara with unnecessary vigour. If he hadn't held her quite so tightly, if she hadn't felt his hands through her dress, if he hadn't smiled down at her like that, she wouldn't be wondering what it would be like if they really were lovers. What it would be like if she could walk out of here and know that he would be waiting for her, that he would open his arms so that she could burrow into the hard strength of his body, that he would draw her down onto the bed and smile against her skin.

A long, slow shiver shuddered its way down Polly's spine and she bent quickly over the basin to splash her face with cold water. It was about time she stopped *wondering*, she told herself firmly. Wondering would only spoil things. Pretending to be in love with Simon was a role she had to play and she would play it as she had agreed, but she had better not forget that it *was* just a role.

Later, when Polly looked back on those two weeks in Provence, she remembered the days as golden ones, long and hot and lazy and suffused with the scent of lavender and thyme.

She filled the house with flowers, and spent happy hours in the kitchen, cooking leisurely meals which they ate outside under the vine-laden trellis, and letting Simon's comments when he tried to clear up afterwards roll over her unnoticed. His grumbles about her untidiness were increasingly half-hearted. Polly thought of them as background noise, like the ceaseless whirring of cicadas, part of the magic of the place which was slowly but surely entwining itself around her heart.

If it hadn't been for the nights, everything would have been perfect. During the day, Polly could forget that she was a convenient stand-in for Simon's fiancée. She got so used to her role that when Simon put his hand against her back, or ran his finger down her cheek, she could respond quite naturally. If he was sitting down, she could go up behind him without thinking and rest her hands on his shoulders. It even felt natural to slide her arms down his chest and stoop to kiss the side of his neck, and in the evenings sometimes she would sit on the floor and lean against Simon's knees and he would stroke her hair, tangling his fingers in its blonde silkiness, and it would feel as if they had always been able to touch each other.

But at night, it was different. Walking through the bedroom door was like stepping from one reality into another. By day, their relationship was warm and natural. They talked and they laughed and they teased each other just as they would have done if they had been lovers. By night, the easy intimacy evaporated into a cool, careful wariness and the air would jangle with a tension that neither of them was prepared to acknowledge.

Polly would lie awake next to Simon and wonder how something that could feel so right could feel so excruciatingly uncomfortable the moment they were alone in the bedroom. It was partly her fault, she knew. Sometimes she would look back at the day and remember how unthinkingly she had taken his hand or leant against him, and, terrified that Simon would begin to think that she was taking the whole pretence a little too seriously, she would retreat behind a barrier of brittle politeness as soon as the bedroom door closed.

It was all right as long as the tension was confined to the times they were alone at night, but as the days passed it began to seep gradually into the day. They tried hard to ignore it, and both did their best to behave exactly as they had done before, but it wasn't easy.

Sometimes it worked. There were times when Polly wondered if she was just imagining that tightness in the air, that way in which Simon was careful not to touch her at all. Times like the ones when they swam in the pool, pretending that no time had passed since they were children and could fool around having water fights.

And then even that respite was gone. Chantal and Julien were setting out lunch in the shade one day, leaving Polly and Simon in the pool. Polly was relaxed and happy, exhilarated by the sun that beat down on her shoulders and glinted off the water and the fact that Simon, too, seemed to be off guard for the day.

Calling his name, she splashed him and dived away before he could retaliate, but he caught up with her easily, pulling her under the water as punishment before they burst to the surface together, laughing, breathless. Polly was clutching at his shoulders and his hands were at her waist, ready to toss her into the air. He had begun to lift her before they realised at the same moment just how close they were, and their smiles faded slowly as the air evaporated between them.

Polly looked down into Simon's face and at the expression in his eyes something began to beat insistently, urgently, inside her. She was preternaturally aware of everything about him, the creases in his cheek, the fan of lines at the corner of his eyes, the droplet trickling between his temple and his jaw. Of the feel of his bare skin, brown and sleek, beneath her fingers, and his hands hard at her waist.

The sunshine glanced off the water, and the reflected light rocked over their glistening bodies, swaying from his back to her shoulders and back over his arm as if they were one. Very slowly, Simon lowered her until her feet touched the bottom of the pool, sliding her down his body, her thigh against his thigh, her stomach against his, her breasts against his chest, and for Polly it was as if time itself had stopped.

It was as if an invisible barrier had dropped, sealing them off from the rest of the world. Beyond it, Chantal and Julien still talked, oblivious to what was happening in the pool, the cicadas still shrilled, the heat still shimmered off the paving stones, but in the water there was only the feel of Simon's body and the light in his eyes and an overwhelming, drumming sense of inevitability.

Wordless, unsmiling, they stared at each other. Day after day, night after night, this was where that terrible tension had been leading, this was what they had been thinking about all along. Polly could feel their resistance splintering like a tangible thing, and her bones liquefied with anticipation and relief that the moment had come at last.

This would be a real kiss. This time she wouldn't be able to claim that she was pretending. Polly didn't care. She didn't want to think about afterwards. All she wanted was the feel of Simon's mouth coming down on hers.

So sure was she that it would happen that her hands were sliding up to his shoulders when, like a blow, Simon shoved her away from him so roughly that she stumbled and fell back into the water.

'It's time for lunch,' he said curtly, turning his back and swinging himself out of the pool. 'Chantal and Julien will be waiting for us.'

CHAPTER NINE

POLLY stood in the water that still rocked from Simon's departure and watched him go, sick with a jarring sense of disbelief and frustration. He had been going to kiss her, he had *wanted* to kiss her, she had seen it in his eyes. Why had he pushed her away as if the feel of her disgusted him? Why had he gone without a word of explanation or apology?

The bitter disappointment that tore at her gave way abruptly before a surge of humiliation as she thought of how she had slid her hands invitingly over his shoulders. She had been practically *begging* him to kiss her. Polly burned, remembering the look on Simon's face as he had thrust her away. He didn't need to explain anything. It was obvious that he had momentarily forgotten who she was and had only just realised that she was the last girl he would want to kiss unless it was absolutely necessary!

Perilously close to tears, Polly made herself swim shakily up and down the pool. She could hear Simon talking to Chantal and Julien on the terrace. He sounded so normal that anger washed through her, and she seized on it as a welcome antidote to the churning embarrassment. Dammit, she had a right to be angry! It wasn't her fault that he had been going to kiss her. He was the one who had started it, she told herself furiously. If he hadn't wanted to kiss her, he should never have held her like that, never have looked at her like that, should never have made her feel like that.

149

'Polly! Lunch is ready,' called Chantal from the terrace.

'Coming!'

Polly towelled herself dry and pulled on a loose shirt to protect her skin from the sun. Her legs felt unsteady, but she couldn't skulk in the pool all day, and she was going to have to face people some time. Clearly, she didn't measure up to Helena or Chantal, and she didn't want to. If Simon didn't want to kiss her, that was fine by *her*!

Taking a deep breath, Polly climbed the steps to the terrace with her head held high.

She ignored Simon over lunch, a task made easier by the fact that he was obviously intent on ignoring her too. He sat as far away from her as possible and devoted himself to Chantal, leaning intimately towards her, making her laugh, smiling at her in a way Polly could only describe as fatuous.

Not that *she* cared! Shaking back her hair, she turned to Julien with a brilliant smile.

Her smile burned at the edges of Simon's vision, and he forced himself not to look at her. Couldn't she see how hard he was trying not to think about her, not to remember the feel of her wet skin beneath his hands?

Simon was still shaken off balance by how nearly he had lost control. It wasn't fair of Polly to sit there now and smile as if nothing *had* happened, he thought resentfully. Of course, nothing had happened, but it was no thanks to her! Why couldn't she go back to being the old irritating, easy-to-ignore Polly? Why did she have to start looking at him with those great blue eyes and sliding her hands up his chest as if she didn't know exactly what she was doing to him? Why did she have to *be* the way she was?

The two weeks were almost over, thought Simon, deliberately feeding his resentment so that he didn't have to think about what would have happened if he had succumbed to temptation in the pool. Why did Polly have to spoil things now?

'Julien, why don't you help me clear away?' Chantal got to her feet as soon as they had finished eating, obviously sensitive to the atmosphere between Simon and Polly and deciding that it would be tactful to leave them alone.

'Leave those, Chantal! You've done enough today.' Polly watched sourly as Simon leapt up. He couldn't have his precious Chantal carrying dirty dishes around, could he? 'Come on, Polly,' he said crossly. 'We'll do this.'

What he meant, of course, was *you'll* do this, thought Polly, sullenly loading glasses into the dishwasher.

'How could you sit there and let Chantal do everything?' Simon snapped as he brought in the last bowls from the table. 'She's supposed to be here on holiday.'

'She only got lunch.' Polly banged plates together as she shoved them into their slots. 'I've done dinner just about every night, in case you've forgotten!'

'And you're being paid for it,' he snarled back, 'in case *you've* forgotten *that*!'

'How could I forget? You don't think I'd have been slaving away and sleeping with you every night unless I was being paid for it, do you?'

Simon was very pale about the mouth. He wasn't about to get into an argument about who had disliked sleeping together the most. Banging the bowls down on the drainer, he snatched the last plates out of Polly's hands.

'Look, there are crumbs everywhere!' he said furiously, taking out his irritation on a safer topic. 'No wonder Martine Sterne sacked you, you can't even load a dishwasher properly! Why can't you rinse them before you stack them?'

'Because only boring, repressed people like you and Helena do that!' she retorted, glad of the invigorating anger that coursed through her veins which made it easy to ignore the terrible urge to throw herself into his arms and burst into tears.

'Helena is the last person you could ever call repressed.' Simon scowled. 'She's got a healthy attitude to everything, and that includes having a sense of hygiene which seems to have passed *you* by!'

'Oh, really? What a pity she's not here, then!'

'Yes, it is a pity,' Simon agreed savagely.

If Helena had been here, he wouldn't have had to spend the last two weeks being distracted and infuriated. He could have concentrated on talking business with Julien instead of wondering where Polly was and what she was doing.

If Helena had come, he would never have noticed the apricot glow of Polly's skin. He wouldn't have recognised her perfume drifting in the air after she had left a room or learnt how her mouth curved into a smile as she slept. His life wouldn't have been turned upside down and he wouldn't be standing here now, not knowing whether he wanted to shake Polly or to kiss her.

'Things might have been a bit more sophisticated if Helena had been able to come,' he said. 'She wouldn't have turned the house into a pit and we could have had some intelligent conversation for a change!'

Polly's eyes flashed dangerously. 'Yes, what stimulating, sophisticated discussions you could have had about loading the dishwasher—' She broke off as the phone on the wall beside her rang, and she snatched up the receiver. If this was Helena, she would tell her just what she could do with her plate-rinsing technique!

'Yes?' she said tightly, and then her face changed. 'Oh...*Philippe*! How lovely to hear from you. I was just thinking about you.' Her eyes met Simon's with open defiance, and his jaw tightened as she lowered her voice intimately while making sure that he could hear every word.

'No, of course I haven't forgotten,' she cooed. '*I'm* certainly coming. I'm looking forward to it...what? No, of course not...' She laughed deliberately. 'Does that mean your offer to teach me French is still open?' she asked without taking her eyes from Simon's. 'Good... I can't wait... I'll see you tomorrow, then.'

Polly pressed the button to cut the connection. 'That was Philippe.'

'No! Was it?' said Simon sarcastically.

'He rang specially to remind me about the party tomorrow night.'

Simon scowled. 'Tomorrow is Chantal and Julien's last day. I thought we would go out for a meal tomorrow night.'

'Fine, we can go to the party afterwards.'

'They may not want to go to a party.'

She shrugged. 'Then I'll go on my own. Suits me.'

Simon's face darkened. 'There's no point in me having endured the last two weeks with you if you're going to throw it away at the end! Chantal and Julien are bound to suspect something's wrong if you insist on swanning off on your own.'

'And there's no point in me having endured the last

two weeks with *you* if I have to pass up this chance to see Philippe again,' Polly pointed out tartly.

'All right.' Simon controlled his temper with an effort. 'But if you go, we all go, and you'd better stick with our story,' he warned. 'We're engaged until Sunday. Chantal and Julien will be gone then, and I'm going back to London as soon as I can, and it can't come soon enough for me. You can do whatever you like after that.'

'Believe me, I can't wait!' snapped Polly.

Sunday…that meant only another day by the pool, only two more mornings when she would wake to the sunlight striping through the shutters and wander barefoot down onto the terrace.

Only two more nights lying next to Simon.

He was obviously longing to get back to Helena. Polly told herself she was glad. She had had enough of being carped at and criticised and ordered around by him. Let Simon go home to Helena and wash up just the way he wanted. She had more exciting plans. She would be free, she would have fun. She would have everything she'd always wanted.

Polly tried hard to whip up some enthusiasm for the prospect as she got ready to go out the next evening. She had always wanted to go to a glamorous party. It would be full of men wearing white dinner jackets and beautiful women whose photographs crowded the glossy magazines. There would be dancing and paparazzi and a whiff of dissolute living.

And she would be there. Polly looked at her reflection and wondered why she felt sick inside. She had put on her best short red dress and the shoes that had pinched her toes so badly the night Simon had turned up at the Sternes' party. Her feet had recovered since then and tonight she wouldn't be waitressing. She would be one of the guests. She would be the one to take a glass from the tray without looking to see who was holding it.

She should be excited. Philippe would be there and he had said that he would be looking out for her. Polly practised a smile at her reflection, but it didn't look natural. She would have to do better than that! She was supposed to be happy; she *was* happy. All she had to do now was to convince Simon just how happy she was.

Simon was prowling around the room behind her, doing up his cuffs. She was going to a lot of trouble for Philippe, he thought morosely. The silky material of her dress slithered over her back as Polly leant forward to stroke mascara carefully onto her lashes, and Simon felt his body clench. What would it be like if he could go over and put his hands on her bare shoulders and let his thumbs caress the nape of her neck, if she tilted her head back and smiled up at him and said that she didn't want to go out at all?

But of course she wouldn't say that. She was longing to go out. This was her big chance to impress Philippe Ladurie, and she was obviously determined to take it.

As if to underline the point, Polly got up and smoothed down her dress as she turned to face him. 'How do I look?' she asked with a brittle smile.

She looked beautiful. 'Fine,' said Simon.

'Do you think Philippe will like my hair up like this?'

How was he supposed to know what Philippe would like? Simon thought savagely. 'I imagine so,' he said.

'I hope you're not going to be as rude to him as you were last time,' Polly warned. 'I don't want you spoiling things for me. I don't mind pretending to be engaged for another night, but there's no need for you to play the jealous fiancé this time.'

Simon looked away. 'No, I won't do that,' he said.

Polly was the life and soul of the party over dinner in the restaurant. Her eyes were very bright and there was a feverish edge to her laughter, but Simon knew that she was just excited at the prospect of seeing Philippe again. He watched her across the table as she lifted her glass and smiled at Julien, and knew with a sudden, stark certainty how much he loved her.

When had he lost control of his feelings for her? When had he learnt to treasure the gleaming laughter in her blue eyes, the curve of her lips as she smiled, the way her hair shimmered when she turned her head?

Simon's mouth twisted at the bitter realisation that this would be the last time he would see her like this. He wanted to drag her out of the restaurant, to take her back to La Treille and beg her to stay, but what would be the point? Polly wanted glamour and excitement. She didn't want to spend the rest of her life with a man who lectured her about washing up. Tomorrow she would be gone, and he would go home and try to tell himself that he liked living in a tidy house again.

'Simon? Are you all right?' Chantal laid a hand on his arm and he started.

'I'm fine.' He mustered a smile. 'If you still want to go to the party, we should think about going.'

He looked at Polly as he spoke, willing her to say that she had changed her mind and that she didn't want to go after all, but she only hesitated long enough to let him hope before she got to her feet with a bright smile.

'I'm ready,' she said. 'Let's party!'

The party was everything Polly had imagined it to be and Philippe even more handsome than she remembered. He welcomed her with flattering warmth, but all Polly noticed was that Simon was apparently happy to stand by and let her be kissed by another man.

It should have been Polly's dream evening. She was at the kind of party she had only ever read about in the gossip columns, surrounded by famous faces, monopolised by the handsomest man there…and she was hating it.

Only half listening to Philippe, she scanned the crowds for Simon, not knowing whether to be hurt or angry at the way he had handed her over to Philippe like a parcel and then disappeared. Every now and then she caught a glimpse of him deep in conversation, but, no matter how hard she laughed and chatted and flirted with Philippe, he didn't even glance in her direction.

The next thing she knew, Simon was leaving with Chantal and Julien. Polly watched them heading for the door in disbelief. He was just going to abandon her here!

Barely bothering to murmur an excuse to Philippe, she fought her way through the crowds to catch Simon's arm at the front door. 'Where are you going?' she demanded furiously.

'Chantal's tired,' he said, glancing over his shoulder to make sure Chantal and Julien were out of earshot. 'They've got to drive back to Paris tomorrow, so I said I'd take them home.'

'What about me?'

'I assumed you'd want to stay,' said Simon in a cool voice. 'You seem to be having a good time with Philippe, and you asked me not to cramp your style so I thought you'd prefer it if we all went away. There's no reason why you shouldn't tell Philippe the truth now, if that's what you want.'

To her horror, Polly realised that she was close to tears. 'You might have told me that you were going.'

'I didn't think you'd notice,' he said bleakly. 'Whenever I looked at you, you were all over Philippe. He seems very taken with you,' he made himself add.

'Yes,' said Polly in a flat voice.

'You must be pleased everything's turning out the way you wanted it to.'

'Yes,' she said again.

There was a pause. Chantal and Julien had stopped and turned to see what had happened to Simon. He lifted a hand to let them know that he was coming and turned back to Polly. 'I'd hoped that you would want to come back to La Treille tonight so that you could say goodbye to Chantal and Julien in the morning, but if things are going so well that you want to stay I'm sure I could think of an excuse for you.'

'No!' said Polly quickly. 'I mean, no, of course I'll come home.'

'I'll come and pick you up in a couple of hours, then.'

A couple of hours! Couldn't he see that she was desperate to go home? That she was tired and miserable and all she wanted was to be taken back to La Treille and go to bed?

'Fine,' she said instead with a brittle smile.

The next two hours were purgatory. Philippe was very attentive, taking her to dance and plying her with champagne, but all Polly could think about was how long it would be before Simon came back for her. She tried to stand where she could keep an eye on the door, terrified that she would miss him.

She saw him the moment he came through the door, cool, contained, unfazed by the growing wildness of the party. Compared to the other men there, he was an understated figure, but as soon as she caught sight of him the air evaporated from Polly's lungs, and her heart gave a great lurch.

He was looking around for her. Quickly, Polly turned back to Philippe and smiled brilliantly up at him, determined that Simon should think that she had spent the most wonderful two hours of her life. She even managed not to jump when Simon appeared at her side and touched her arm.

'Oh, there you are,' she said as casually as she could.

'Are you ready to go?'

'Already?' As if she hadn't spent the whole evening longing to leave!

'I'll wait outside if you want.'

'I might as well come now,' said Polly hastily.

'I'll meet you at the car, then,' he said, not even waiting to see her say goodbye to Philippe.

Blinking back tears of tiredness and disappointment, Polly followed him. Her head was aching and her feet hurt, and all she wanted right then was his arm to support her to the car.

'Did you have a good time?' Simon asked her as she got in beside him.

'Fantastic!' she lied. Her voice felt high and strained. 'I didn't realise Philippe was so funny. He made me laugh all evening. We spent the whole time dancing and talking—it was so romantic! He's so nice, too, really warm and interested. I feel as if I know him so much better now.' Polly could her herself rattling but couldn't seem to stop. 'He said he liked my hair and he remembered my shoes from last time.'

Simon kept his eyes on the road. 'Did you tell him that we weren't really engaged?'

'Not exactly. I said that we were having problems, so I don't think he'll be surprised when I tell him it's all off. He did say that if I ever needed anywhere to stay I could stay with him. All I have to do is give him a ring.'

Simon's knuckles were white against the steering wheel. 'Is that what you're going to do tomorrow?'

'I…well, I…I suppose so.' Polly stammered to a halt, as the truth hit her at last. She didn't want to go anywhere. She wanted to stay at La Treille, with Simon.

Slowly, she turned to look at him. His face was shadowed, underlit by the glow from the dashboard, and the realisation of how much she loved him crashed over her like a great, rolling, breaking wave, leaving her gasping and disorientated and struggling to find her feet in the terrifying undertow.

So this was it. Polly had always rather looked forward to falling in love, but she hadn't expected it to feel like this. She had imagined herself fierily passionate or glowing with contentment, not gripped by this turbulent mixture of joy and despair that churned and swirled and changed everything. Love might not be how she had imagined it to be, but Polly knew with a sickening certainty that love was what it was, and there was nothing she could do about it.

I love you.

The impulse to blurt out the truth was so strong that she had to lift a hand to her mouth to push back the words. Of course she loved him, but how could she tell him now? How could she ever tell him?

Simon loved Helena, not her. Polly looked at his

drawn face and belatedly tried to understand what a strain the last two weeks must have been for him. She had told him that she was in love with Philippe, but that had just been a fantasy. His love for Helena was a real thing.

It couldn't have been easy for him to pretend to be in love with her, knowing that Helena was back in London. How he must have missed Helena's calm, serene presence! It wasn't even as if Simon had tried to hide how he felt about her. He had told Polly often enough how perfect Helena was, and how well they got on together. He wasn't going to give that up for a girl like Polly, who was disorganised and messy and who did nothing but irritate him and argue with him.

Swallowing, Polly wrenched her eyes away from his face and looked out of her window at the darkness rushing by. No, she could never tell Simon that she loved him. At best, he would be kind, at the worst contemptuous, and either way would only lead to acute embarrassment for them both. If he had been a stranger, she might have taken the risk, but Simon was part of the family. She would have to get used to seeing him with Helena, she would have to go to his wedding and smile and pretend that her heart wasn't breaking.

Terrified that Simon would read the longing in her eyes, Polly averted her face as they went inside. Chantal and Julien were asleep, and she was glad of the excuse not to turn on the lights. She went quickly upstairs to the bedroom and fled to the bathroom, shutting herself in and staring at her desperate reflection in the mirror while she found the courage to climb into bed beside him knowing that it would be for the last time.

In the bedroom, Simon cursed softly to himself as

he undressed. Everything had gone wrong. He had hoped that if he gave Polly the chance to spend a whole evening with Philippe, she might discover that she wasn't in love with him after all, but instead it had had the opposite effect. Judging by what she had said in the car, she was obviously still mad about him.

And there was absolutely nothing he could do about it. Simon's face was grim as he unfastened his shirt. She could hardly wait to ring Philippe up and take him up on his offer of a place to stay, and once she was there she wouldn't be able to resist his practised charms for long, even if she wanted to. Which she didn't, Simon reminded himself bleakly.

He was going to have to let her go, even though every fibre of his being rebelled at the prospect. Philippe wouldn't make her happy. Couldn't she see that he didn't really care about her? He didn't know how warm and funny and exasperating she was, he hadn't seen her grow from a naughty little girl into an exasperating teenager before blossoming into the beautiful woman she was now. His heart didn't turn over every time she turned her head and smiled, or lifted her face to the sunlight.

No, Simon was convinced that all Philippe knew was that she had long legs and apparently belonged to another man. That would be all it took to pique the interest of a man like that. Engaged to another man, Polly was a challenge; alone, she would have little to offer Philippe and Simon was desperately afraid that she would be hurt.

And if she was, he would be around to pick up the pieces, Simon vowed fiercely. He could easily make an excuse to stay down here for a while. If she needed him, he would be here for her. If not...

If not, he would have to go back to London and get on with life without her.

The bathroom door opened, and Polly appeared, just as she had done every night for the last two weeks, long legs bare beneath the faded baggy T-shirt she wore in place of a nightdress, face scrubbed clean and blonde hair falling over her shoulders. And Simon's throat tightened at the sight of her, just as it had done every night for the last two weeks.

His hands fell from his shirt as he looked at her. It was the first time that he had seen her face clearly since he'd picked her up from the party, and, having braced himself for shining happiness, he was thrown off balance by the strained look in her eyes. He frowned. 'Is something wrong, Polly?'

Everything was wrong, thought Polly desolately.

It wasn't fair of Simon to stand there with his shirt unfastened. His chest was broad and inviting. It would be so easy to walk over and lean against it, to rest her face at his throat and wrap her arms around his back, to feel the steady, reassuring beat of his heart and breathe in the clean, comfortingly male scent of his skin. Polly wanted it so badly that tears stung her eyes and she had to force her feet in the opposite direction.

'No,' she said brightly, sitting on her side of the bed with her back to him. 'I'm just a bit tired, that's all. It's been an exciting evening.'

She wished that he hadn't looked at her with such concern, as if he could see that her heart was cracking and awash with longing. She didn't want him to feel guilty because he couldn't love her as she loved him. He had given her what he thought she wanted, and now she would do the same for him. He needed to be able to go home to Helena without worrying about her being alone and unhappy in France, or being afraid that she would embarrass him or make a fuss. All she had to do was convince him that she was fine.

'What could be wrong?' she went on, flashing him a smile over her shoulder. 'I've been dancing all night with the handsomest man I've ever seen, and I'm going to see him again tomorrow.'

'It looks like you'll have that great, romantic affair you wanted, after all,' said Simon heavily.

'Yes,' said Polly, but it was a relief when he switched the lights out and she could stop smiling.

'Goodbye, Polly.' Chantal gave her a warm hug. 'Thank you so much for all those wonderful meals!'

'I wish you didn't have to go,' said Polly, meaning it. Even if it hadn't meant the end of her time with Simon, she had grown very fond of Chantal and Julien over the last two weeks.

'We must, I'm afraid,' said Chantal, 'and, in any case, I think it's time you and Simon spent some time on your own.' She smiled at Polly. 'You will let us know when the wedding is, won't you?'

'What wedding?' asked Polly blankly.

Chantal laughed. 'Yours, of course!'

Simon put an arm round Polly at that and held her firmly against him. 'We'll send you an invitation as soon as we've decided on a date.'

The feel of his arm around her was bitter-sweet. This would be the last time they would have to pretend, Polly realised, her last chance to lean into the hard security of his body. Succumbing to temptation, she put her arm around his waist and hoped that no one could see how desperately she longed to burrow against him and burst into tears.

Julien kissed her affectionately on both cheeks and turned to clap a hand to Simon's shoulder. 'We'll be in touch about the merger,' he promised. 'And don't wait too long to arrange a date for the wedding,' he said, looking seriously from one to the other. 'You belong together.'

Simon and Polly stood with their arms around each other and waved until the car was out of sight. It was almost as if both of them were trying to prolong the moment before they had to step apart and drop the pretence, but at last the car was gone and the sound of the engine had receded into the distance leaving only the whirr of the cicadas and the echo of Julien's words hanging in the hot, still air.

You belong together.

Only they didn't. There was nothing now to stop them dropping their arms, moving away from each other, walking off in different directions.

It was Simon who slackened his hold first, and as soon as she felt it Polly leapt away from him, terrified that he would think that she was clinging. The silence was awful.

'They'll be very disappointed when they hear we're not getting married after all,' she said in a brittle voice at last.

'Yes,' Simon agreed heavily.

'What will you tell them?'

He shrugged. 'I'll say you found someone else. If all goes well with you and Philippe it will be true, anyway.'

There was another agonising pause.

'It'll be a relief to stop pretending, won't it?' Unable to meet his eyes, Polly fiddled with the engagement ring on her finger.

'Yes.'

'You don't need me any more.'

Simon hesitated, and she held her breath, but in the end all he said was, 'No.'

Struggling to master the bitter disappointment, Polly tugged the ring off her finger. 'You might as well have this back, then,' she said bleakly as she held it out to him.

He didn't take it immediately. 'Are you sure you don't want to keep it?'

'Yes.' She nodded. 'An engagement ring is something special. This one is just a prop. The next time I wear a ring on this finger, I want it to be for real.' She swallowed. 'I don't want to pretend any more.' Which was ironic, she thought wearily, given that all she was doing now was pretending not to be in love with him.

'OK.' Simon took the ring brusquely from her and shoved it into his pocket. 'Do you want to ring Philippe now?'

'I…I'd rather do it from town.' Polly was very close to tears. She took a steadying breath and mustered a smile from somewhere. 'Do you think you could give me a lift with my case?'

'Of course.' They were both being carefully polite. Simon forced an answering smile. 'You must be anxious to go as soon as possible.'

No! Polly wanted to shout. I don't want to go at all! I want to stay here with you!

'Yes,' she said instead. 'I'll go and pack now.'

CHAPTER TEN

SIMON had insisted on buying her a suitcase in Marsillac on one of their shopping trips. Polly packed it slowly, her throat tight with the effort of not crying. Everything she put in seemed to remind her of a time with Simon, a time when she hadn't known that she loved him and had been happy.

He was waiting for her as she carried the case down the stairs. His face was set, his mouth a bleak line. 'Have you got everything?'

'I think so.' She summoned a smile. 'I've tried not to leave any mess.'

'Ready to go, then?'

Afraid to trust her voice, Polly nodded.

She didn't let herself look back at La Treille as she walked out and got into the car, but when Simon drove out along the track and onto the road she felt as if she were being torn away like a limpet from a rock.

The drive into town was an agony. Polly longed for it to be over, but dreaded it at the same time. The prospect of saying goodbye to Simon was stuck painfully in her throat, and tears prickled at the back of her eyes, no matter how often she swallowed them down. She couldn't have spoken if she had tried.

Simon insisted on going to a bank, where he drew out what seemed to Polly to be a huge sum of money and handed it over to her. 'It's too much,' she protested.

'It's what we agreed.'

Polly took the money reluctantly. 'I didn't do anything to deserve all this. I've just been on holiday for two weeks.'

'You cooked and you made Chantal and Julien welcome, and you convinced them we were engaged. You did everything you said you'd do. You earned that money, Polly,' said Simon. 'It's yours now to do whatever you want.'

She bit her lip, suspecting that he had given her much more than she needed, but they couldn't stand here throwing money at each other all day. She would take what she thought she had earned and give the rest to her father to return to Simon later. 'All right...thank you,' she said and put the notes in her purse as she followed him out of the bank.

Simon had been carrying the case, but he handed it to her on the wide pavement under the plane trees in an oddly formal gesture, as if he were giving up far more than a suitcase.

'Well,' said Polly bravely, putting the case down and squaring her shoulders. 'I guess this is it.'

Simon's face was strained. 'I want you to promise me something,' he said abruptly.

'What?'

'If things don't work out, if you need anything—anything at all—I want you to let me know. I'm going to stay at La Treille for a while, so you know where to find me.'

She looked at him in surprise, startled out of her misery. 'I thought you were going back to London.'

'I was but...' Simon didn't want to tell her that he was afraid that Philippe would hurt her and wanted to be around to comfort her '...I changed my mind,' he finished lamely.

There was a tiny pause. 'It'll be lonely on your own,' said Polly in a tight voice, hoping against hope that he would admit it and ask her to stay to keep him company for a while.

'I'll ring Helena.' He had to convince Polly that his offer to help her was disinterested. If she even guessed that he had fallen in love with her, she would run a mile from the awkwardness of the situation.

'She should have finished her job by now,' he ploughed on. 'Maybe she'll come down for a few days and we can have a proper holiday together.'

'Good idea,' said Polly, wondering why he couldn't hear her heart splintering.

Simon tried hard to hide the urgency in his voice. 'So you will ring me if you need anything?'

'I can't imagine that I'll need anything with all the money you've just given me—' she began, but he interrupted her before she could finish.

'Promise me anyway.'

'All right.' She swallowed. 'I promise.'

They looked at each other. There was a leaden feeling in Simon's stomach. He was going to have to let her go.

'Goodbye, Polly,' he heard himself say. His voice sounded as if it belonged to someone else. 'Thanks for everything.'

Polly couldn't speak. She could only look back at him with dark blue eyes, and Simon put his arms around her and pulled her against him in a desperate hug. As a friend of the family, he was allowed to do that, surely? He didn't dare let himself kiss her, though, not even on the cheek. All he could do was hold her tightly and rest his cheek against her silky hair for the last time.

'Good luck,' he said hoarsely.

Polly clung to him. 'Goodbye,' she whispered as he released her, and, bending to pick up her case so that he wouldn't see the tears in her eyes, she turned and walked quickly away without once looking back.

'Why are you doing this to yourself, Polly?' Philippe sat down next to her and put an arm round her shoulders.

In the three days since she had arrived on his doorstep with an expression of stark misery, Philippe had proved himself kinder than Polly had ever imagined, dropping his façade of suave sophistication as soon as he'd seen how unhappy she was and devoting himself instead to cheering her up. Polly did her best to repay his generosity by being bright and cheerful, but she obviously wasn't fooling Philippe. 'You don't want to be here,' he told her gently.

'I'm sorry.' Her face crumpled and she shook her head as if it would be enough to stop the tears spilling down her cheeks. 'I shouldn't have come here. I was hoping that I'd fall in love with you...' she confessed miserably.

'But you're still in love with Simon?' Philippe finished for her, and she nodded helplessly.

Philippe produced a clean white handkerchief and handed it to her. 'I think you'd better tell me all about it,' he said.

His sympathy was the last straw. Polly broke down and wept into his handkerchief, and gradually Philippe coaxed the whole story out of her. 'Good girl,' he said, patting her shoulder when she had sobbed her way to the end. 'Now all you've got to do is go and tell Simon what you've just told me!'

'I c-can't!'

'Of course you can,' said Philippe bracingly. 'You seem very certain that he doesn't love you, but I'm not sure. No one can act that well! He sounds to me like a man in love and trying to deny it, just like you've been doing.'

'Really?' Hope glimmered in Polly's tear-drenched eyes.

'There's only one way to find out.' Philippe got up and stretched down a hand to pull her to her feet. 'Simon made you promise to go to him if you ever needed him, and you do, don't you?'

'Yes.' Polly's smile was rather watery as she kissed him on the cheek. 'You've been so kind, Philippe!'

'It's a new role for me,' he confessed with a wry look. 'Usually I am the one making the girls cry because I don't love them. It makes a nice change for me to be the good guy for once! Now, come on and I'll drive you back to La Treille.'

The wind blew Polly's hair around her face as Philippe drove his open-topped Mercedes coupé back towards the town, and hope warred with panic in her heart. She had no idea what she was going to say to Simon when she saw him.

But as it turned out she didn't see him and there was no need to say anything. She saw Helena instead.

They had to go through the town to pick up the road to La Treille, and the car was sitting at traffic lights near the main square when Helena came out of a *boulangerie* carrying a baguette and a box of pastries. Polly had only met her once, but she recognised her instantly and a cold hand closed around her heart.

Their eyes met and she could see Helena frown, obviously trying to work out where she had seen her before. Simon must have rung her as soon as he had got home, and Helena had come as soon as he had called. Polly's heart twisted. Of course she had. The two of them belonged together. They had La Treille and the hot days and the long nights all to themselves, and the last thing they needed was Polly turning up on the doorstep, desperate to believe that Simon might magically fall out of love with Helena and in love with her.

'Philippe?' said Polly in frozen voice.

'Yes?'

She moistened her lips. 'I've changed my mind about going to La Treille. Would you take me to the station instead?'

'You're very quiet, Polly.' Polly's mother looked at her in concern as they walked towards the church in the crisp autumn sunshine. 'Is something the matter?'

'Of course not, Mum. It was a long journey back from Nice yesterday, that's all.'

Her mother squeezed her arm. 'I'm so glad you made it back for Charlie's wedding. All the Taverners were saying it wouldn't be the same if you weren't here today.'

All of them? Polly wondered. 'I suppose Simon will be here,' she said with studied casualness, although it still hurt just to say his name.

'Of course.' Frances Armstrong looked at her daughter in surprise. 'He'd hardly miss his brother's wedding!'

'I hope you're going to be nice to him for once,' her father put in. 'Simon went out of his way to see that you were all right in France. It was a great relief to us when he came back and told us that you were fine and had just been working hard, but he didn't say much else and we were afraid you might have been rude to him like you usually are!'

Polly swallowed. 'I wasn't rude,' she said in a low voice.

'I'm glad to hear it,' said her mother. 'Simon's not himself at the moment at all.' She lowered her voice conspiratorially. 'Margaret thinks he's in love!'

Claws of pain raked across Polly's heart and she bent, pretending to shake a pebble from her shoe so that her parents wouldn't see her face. She had spent the last three months trying to convince herself that she wasn't really in love with Simon. She had told herself that it was no more than an infatuation, that she had been carried away by the beauty of Provence and the romance of the situation, but it hadn't stopped her missing Simon every single day with a raw, desperate need.

She wasn't sure that she was ready to see him again yet, especially not with Helena, but she had promised Charlie a long time ago that she would be at his wedding. Deep down, she had been hoping that as soon as she laid eyes on Simon she would discover that the magic had somehow gone, but, judging by the way she flinched in pain at the mere mention of his name, it wasn't going to work.

Circling around the edge of the group of guests greeting each other with much kissing and hugging outside the church, Polly tried to make sure that she saw Simon before he saw her so that she could brace herself for the meeting. There seemed to be no sign of him, though. Polly veered from nervousness to frustration to panic in case he wasn't there after all and then, just when she had given up, he came out of the church porch with his brother.

She had expected to find the first meeting difficult, but she was still unprepared for the way a mere glimpse of him thumped into her, like a fist into her stomach, sending the air whooshing out of her lungs. She drank in the sight of him, longing to touch him but terrified that if he came anywhere near her she would fall apart and embarrass everybody, and as he began to turn in her direction she ducked quickly behind a gravestone, glad of the hat that shaded her face.

She couldn't see any sign of Helena. She was probably inside the church already, Polly decided. Helena was the kind of girl who would make sure that she had a good seat wherever she was.

Unsure whether to be disappointed or relieved that Simon made no effort to seek her out, Polly slipped into a pew beside her parents where she could watch the back of his head. He was sitting next to a woman in a spectacular hat. Helena? It was difficult to tell from behind.

The bridal march began with a flourish, and Polly's heart cracked at the simple love and pride in Charlie's face as he turned to watch his bride coming up the aisle towards him. If only she could imagine a time when Simon would look at her like that!

Desperately conscious of Simon two rows in front of her, Polly found the wedding service unbearably poignant, and the tears streamed silently down her face until her mother leant round her father and handed her a tissue with a worried look.

It was easy enough to avoid Simon while the photographs were being taken and it was only during the reception that Polly began to suspect that he might be avoiding her too. He always seemed to be at the other side of the room. She tried not to watch him, but she was achingly aware of every move he made. Bright smile pinned onto her face, Polly chatted dutifully and drank champagne and noticed every time Simon turned his head or smiled or lifted his glass.

Why didn't he come over and say hello? They had been friends, hadn't they? She hadn't embarrassed him and she had gone when he had wanted. Didn't he know how much she longed just to be close to him?

'What's going on between you and Simon?' Polly was startled out of her thoughts as Emily dragged her aside.

'What do you mean?'

'You keep looking at each other when you think the other one's not looking.'

Involuntarily Polly looked across the room just as Simon glanced towards her and their eyes met for a jarring moment before both looked quickly away.

'Like that,' said Emily.

Polly laughed unconvincingly. 'Nothing's going on. Simon's probably just waiting to come over and tell me he disapproves of my outfit.'

Emily raised her brows. Polly was wearing a dusky blue suit with a short skirt and her hair was pinned up under a wide-brimmed hat. 'Even Simon couldn't disapprove of that outfit,' she pointed out. 'It's very restrained for you! Positively grown up! In fact,' she went on slowly, 'you look quite different since you've been in France. What happened to you there?'

I fell in love with your brother. Polly could just imagine Emily's reaction if she told her the truth, so she shrugged instead. 'Must be all that French style rubbing off on me.'

'Perhaps.'

Emily had uncomfortably shrewd eyes sometimes

and Polly tried to divert her. The last thing she wanted was for Emily to suspect that she had a secret. She wouldn't rest until she had uncovered it. 'I was just wondering where Helena was,' she said quickly. It wasn't much of an excuse for watching Simon, but it was the best she could do.

'Helena who?' Emily looked puzzled.

'Helena. Simon's girlfriend.' It hurt Polly just to say it.

'Oh, *her*. God, they haven't been together for ages!'

Polly stared. 'What? Are you sure?'

'Of course I'm sure,' said Emily, affronted. 'I assumed you knew. They broke up…ooh, June some time, I suppose. Before Simon went off to France anyway. I can't say I'm sorry either. I never liked her, did you?'

'No,' said Polly, dry-mouthed. Her heart was beating so hard she could hardly speak. Why hadn't Simon told her about Helena? 'So who's he going out with at the moment?' she asked as casually as she could, praying that the mothers had got it wrong and that the answer would be 'no one'.

'Well, we don't know!' Emily glanced around and leant forward confidingly, unaware that she was dashing Polly's sudden hope. 'But, whoever she is, she's obviously very special! Simon's being very mysterious. He admitted to Mum that he was in love, but then he clammed up and he won't talk to me about it at all,' she added with an air of grievance.

'We're all afraid he knows we won't like her when we meet her. I don't know why he's being so cagey about it,' she grumbled, obviously frustrated at her brother's reticence. 'I mean, I know we think no one would be good enough for him, but we'd make an effort to like anyone he loved enough to marry, wouldn't we?'

'Yes,' Polly agreed dully. 'Of course we would.'

A party was planned for the evening, and by the time the reception was over there was only time to change before they had to start again. The wedding party had booked out the entire hotel, so at least Polly had a room of her own to slip away to if things got too bad. She sat hunched on the bed, hugging her arms to her as if she were cold, and fought down the pain.

Her heart had leapt at the news that Simon had lied to her about Helena, only to crash again as she'd realised that he would have told her the truth if he hadn't wanted her to keep her distance. Or perhaps he had still been in love with Helena and hoping that they would get together again? He had rung her and asked her to come down to La Treille, hadn't he?

And when that hadn't worked, he had found someone else and fallen in love for real.

Polly got stiffly to her feet and told herself to face facts. Simon didn't love her and he never would. Mechanically, she changed into her red dress and put on her make-up. She mustn't spoil Charlie's wedding. All she had to do was get through the evening and then she could cry.

Polly tried that night. She really tried. She smiled. She laughed. She danced. But her smile must have been over-bright and her eyes glittery with unshed tears because just about everyone she talked to looked at her in concern and asked if she was all right.

Just when Polly had given up hoping that Simon would acknowledge her at all, he came over and her heart stopped. She was standing with Emily and one of the Taverner cousins, an irritatingly jolly stockbroker called Giles.

'Hello, Polly,' said Simon.

'Hello.' Her voice cracked, and she could see the others look at her in surprise. 'How have you been?'

'Fine. And you?'

'Fine.'

Emily looked sharply from one to the other, but Giles, notoriously insensitive to atmosphere, simply thumped Simon on the shoulder. 'Time you were getting married too, Simon. Can't have your younger brother and sister showing you up like this!' He guffawed. 'I'm sure we could find you a nice girl to marry. What about Polly here? She's free, aren't you, Polly?' He brayed with laughter again. 'Keep it in the family and save us all a wedding present!'

Emily glanced at Polly to roll her eyes at her cousin's tactlessness, only to surprise such a stricken expression in her friend's face that she caught her breath. 'What's the matter, Pol? Are you ill?'

It was too much for Polly. 'Why do people keep asking me what the matter is?' she cried, teetering on the verge of hysteria. 'There's nothing the matter with me! I'm absolutely fine!' To her horror, her mouth began to tremble and she put up a hand to hide it.

There was a moment of appalled silence, then Simon reached calmly out and took her other hand in a warm clasp. 'Come and dance,' he said, and, without waiting for her to reply, he led her onto the crowded dance floor, leaving Emily and Giles staring open-mouthed after them.

The band was in full flow, but he couldn't resist keeping hold of Polly's hand and putting his other arm around her to pull her close. For comfort, Simon told himself. She was distressed. She needed someone to lean against, and it might as well be him.

It was such a relief just to be able to hold her again. He hadn't dared come near her all day in case he'd succumbed to the temptation to yank her into his arms. She had looked sophisticated and unfamiliar in that smart suit today, but when she had come down this evening in her red dress with her hair tumbled down her back she was so much the Polly he remembered that he hadn't been able to resist any longer.

Closer to, though, she was looking thinner than he liked, and she had lost that sparkle that was so much part of her. Philippe's doing, no doubt, Simon thought savagely. He had known the Frenchman wouldn't be able to make her happy. He should have stayed in France for her, instead of giving up and coming home to be miserable without her.

It was bliss to be with him again. Intensely grateful to Simon for rescuing her from an embarrassing scene, Polly felt the hysteria recede as she gave herself up to the hazy pleasure of being held by him, even if it was just for a few short minutes. She wouldn't think about the fact that he was just being kind. She wouldn't think about how it would feel when he let her go again. She would just think about how good it felt to lean into the hard solidity of his body, to feel his hand, warm and strong, against her back, to know that if she turned her head a tiny bit she could kiss his throat.

They held each other in silence, hardly dancing, hardly aware of the others bopping around the floor in time to the band. Simon felt the tension drain slowly out of Polly and allowed himself to rest his cheek against her hair, breathing in her scent. It was too noisy to talk. He could just hold her. Just for a while.

As if on cue, the band switched to a slow, schmaltzy number, depriving him of his excuse not to talk. Perhaps it was just as well, thought Simon. With Polly warm and pliant in his arms, it would be so easy to let her nearness go to his head and forget the reality that she was unhappy and needed support, not seduction.

'Is it Philippe?' he asked her, an edge of roughness to his voice.

For a moment Polly couldn't think who he was talking about. Puzzled, she pulled away slightly so that she could look into his face. 'Philippe?'

'I was afraid he might have hurt you. I thought that's why you were upset when that idiot Giles started going on about marriage in his usual tactless way.'

'Oh.' Polly assimilated that slowly. 'No, I wasn't upset about Philippe,' she said at last. 'I haven't seen him since June.'

'What?' Simon's hold tightened in shock. 'I thought you'd been with him all this time!'

She shook her head. 'No. I've been in Nice. I got a job as a waitress and I've been there three months.' She managed a smile. 'Quite a record for me, isn't it? My French is quite good now. You'd be proud of me.'

Simon hardly heard her. He was still trying to adjust to the fact that she hadn't spent the summer in Philippe's arms. 'But...but what happened between you and Philippe?'

Polly's gaze slid away from his. 'Oh, it just didn't work out,' she said vaguely. How could she tell Simon that he was the reason she had spent a long, lonely summer while he was busy falling in love with another woman?

And *that* was a subject she might as well face right now.

'How about you?' she asked and forced herself to meet his eyes again with a brilliant smile. 'I hear you're in love?'

Simon seemed to freeze as he looked down into her face. 'Yes, I am,' he said slowly. 'How did you know?'

'Emily told me.' Polly felt as if iron hands were gripping her throat but she refused to cry.

'Ah.' Simon's hold tightened almost absently as he swung her round.

Polly made a superhuman effort to lighten the atmosphere. 'Is she nice?'

'Who?'

'The girl you're in love with.'

'Yes, she is.'

'Pretty?'

Simon looked down into Polly's eyes. 'I think she's beautiful.'

Why was she torturing herself like this? 'She sounds perfect,' she managed.

'No, she's not perfect. There are one or two things about her that drive me crazy, but she's got the warmest smile and the truest eyes and she's the only girl I'll ever want.'

Tears were standing in Polly's eyes. 'Are you going to get married?' she made herself ask, her voice wobbling with the effort of not crying.

'If she'll have me.'

'Haven't you asked her yet?'

'No. Do you think I should?' asked Simon with interest and she bit down hard on her lip.

'If…if you're sure you love her.'

'I am,' he said. 'I'm as sure as I can ever be about anything that I love her and I need her and I want to spend the rest of my life with her.'

How could he do this to her? 'Th-then you should ask her,' said Polly painfully.

'What if she doesn't love me back?'

She looked at him, her eyes shimmering with tears. 'Don't you know?'

'No,' said Simon, 'but if you think I should, I'll ask her anyway.'

The long doors of the hotel ballroom had been opened to let in the cool night air, and he danced with Polly out onto the long terrace. Coming to a halt in the shadows, he released her, but only to take both her hands in a warm clasp.

'Will you marry me, Polly?'

Polly heard the words, but they didn't seem to make sense. Simon couldn't possibly have asked her to marry him when he was in love with someone else. She stared at him, eyes huge and dark in her pale face, and Simon's smile twisted.

'Of course it's you,' he said. 'How could it be anyone else?'

'But you don't love me,' she whispered incredulously.

'I do. I love you more than I can ever tell you,' said Simon. 'I used to think of you as a silly little girl, but when you opened the door at the Sternes' party you'd changed. You weren't a little girl any longer. And then you kissed me.'

He smiled down into Polly's dazed face. 'Do you remember that kiss, Polly? You were so casual about it. For you, it was just an experiment to see if a kiss would make you feel different about me, and as far as you were concerned it failed. But it worked for me. I started falling in love with you right then, and before

I knew where I was I couldn't imagine life without you.'

'B-but...I'm so messy...and disorganised,' she stammered.

'I know,' said Simon, 'but when you'd gone, the house was so empty and lifeless, I couldn't stand it. I'd have done anything to have you back, spreading your things around. I didn't want to fall in love with you, Polly,' he told her slowly. 'I did everything I could to resist it. I was jealous of Philippe, and I knew you could never love me the way I loved you. How could you when I'd done nothing but criticise you and argue with you, and you thought of me as a bossy big brother?'

Somewhere deep inside Polly a smile was trembling into life. She hardly dared believe what she had heard. 'I've never thought of you as my brother, Simon,' she said, amazed to find that her voice was quite steady after all. 'Emily's brother, yes, but not mine.'

'Well, you know what I mean.'

'Yes, I do know what you mean,' said Polly and the smile reached her lips at last. 'I know exactly what you mean. I know what it's like to find that someone you've always taken for granted is suddenly the most important person in your life. I know what it's like to fall in love and not be able to tell that person because you can't believe they could ever be in love with you.'

'Polly...' Simon's fingers tightened around hers. 'Polly, what are you saying?'

'I'm saying that you're wrong.' Her smile wavered and the tears that had been so close all day spilled over in sheer relief at being able to say it at last. 'I can love you the way you love me, and I do...oh, Simon, I do!'

The next moment she found herself swept into
Simon's arms and golden happiness cascaded through
her as he kissed her the way she had dreamed of him
kissing her for so long. It was like coming home after
a dark, desperate journey. Polly put her arms round his
neck and kissed him back, again and again to make
sure that she wasn't dreaming after all.

'Polly,' said Simon unsteadily at last, cupping her
face between his hands and looking down at her with
wonder. 'Say it again, Polly. Tell me that you love me.'

'I love you,' she said simply.

'You once said that when you fell in love it would
be for ever,' he reminded her, and she smiled mistily.

'I know, and I will love you for ever…and you know
I *always* fulfil my contracts!'

Gently, Simon wiped the last traces of tears from her
cheeks with his thumbs. 'So you'll marry me?'

'Yes,' she said simply and he kissed her again.

'I've got something for you,' he said some time later
when he raised his head again, and Polly rested her
face against his throat with a sigh of sheer contentment.
Digging around in his pocket, he pulled out the sapphire and diamond ring that they had bought together
in France.

Polly's eyes were like stars, and his throat tightened
as her face lit with delight. 'My ring!' she said, and
Simon slipped it back where it belonged on her third
finger.

'It's a real engagement ring this time, Polly. I've
been carrying it around ever since you gave it back to
me that day,' he confessed. 'It was all I had of yours.
I'd take it out and hold it and think about you, willing
you to get tired of Philippe and come home so that I
could just see you again.'

'I wish I'd known,' sighed Polly, wrapping her arms more tightly around him. 'We've wasted so much time.'

'I shouldn't have let you go, but you seemed so sure that you wanted to be with Philippe. I hoped that it wouldn't take you long to find out that he wasn't the man for you, and that you'd come back to me, but you didn't.' Simon grimaced as he remembered how empty and echoing the house had been when she had gone.

'I nearly did. Philippe said I should just tell you how I felt, and was driving me over when I saw Helena in the town. I assumed you'd asked her to come down and there didn't seem to be any point in telling you anything then, so I got on the first train that came into the station. I couldn't bear the thought of seeing you and Helena together.'

'I didn't know that you'd seen her,' said Simon slowly. 'That must have been before she arrived at La Treille. She turned up, cool as you like, expecting us to pick up where we'd left off. She'd even brought lunch! She told me that she'd seen you, except that she couldn't remember who you were, so she described you and Philippe. That's how I knew that you were with him.'

He sighed. 'Helena went on and on about it, wondering why you were so familiar and what you were doing in France with such a handsome man, until I could have cheerfully throttled her with her baguette!'

Polly giggled. She could even feel sorry for Helena now. 'So you didn't ring and ask her to come down?'

'Of course not. I'd only said that I was going to do that to give me an excuse to stay nearby in case things didn't work out between you and Philippe. She was the last person I wanted to see right then!'

He held Polly tighter, so happy to know that she loved him that it was hard to remember his despair as he had opened the door and seen Helena standing there instead of her.

'We'd had a big argument before I left. Helena suddenly announced that she wanted to get married and said that she wouldn't go to France unless I was prepared to commit myself to her in some way. I wasn't, and some pretty unpleasant things were said. As far as I was concerned the relationship was over, and I thought it was for Helena, too, but once she'd finished her job she seemed to have decided that all I needed was to get used to the idea.

'It was supposed to be a wonderful surprise when she turned up at La Treille without warning, but all it did was make me realise how much I loved *you*, and how much I was missing you.' He dropped a kiss on her mouth, loving the taste of her, the feel of her, remembering how desperately empty the house had been when she had gone. 'It had been so easy just being with you.'

'It wasn't always easy,' Polly reminded him as she smiled against his throat. 'Lying next to you night after night and not being able to touch you wasn't easy at all!'

'You think I don't know that? If it was bad for you, what do you think it was like for me?' demanded Simon as she began to kiss her way along his jaw.

'It can't have been worse,' she mumbled between kisses. 'If you'd so much as brushed against me, I'd have burst into flames!'

Simon laughed and pressed her back against the wall so that he could kiss her properly, an insistent, intoxicating kiss that went on and on, spinning Polly along in a spiral of mounting desire until she thought that she would dissolve with excitement.

'And now?' he murmured against her lips.

'Now you'll do more than brush, won't you?' she replied in a voice ragged with need.

'I can safely promise you that,' said Simon, smiling in a way that turned her bones to honey. He took her hand and pulled her along the terrace. 'Come on. The party's going strong and no one will miss us if we slip away.'

'Where are we going?'

'We're going to make up for all those nights lying apart,' he said as he produced a key to his hotel room. 'Any objections?'

'No,' said Polly happily as Simon kissed her again and led her towards the lift. 'None at all.'

HARLEQUIN ◆ PRESENTS®

**The world's bestselling romance series...
The series that brings you your favorite authors,
month after month:**

Helen Bianchin...Emma Darcy
Lynne Graham...Penny Jordan
Miranda Lee...Sandra Morton
Anne Mather...Carole Mortimer
Susan Napier...Michelle Reid

and many more uniquely talented authors!

Wealthy, powerful, gorgeous men...
Women who have feelings just like your own...
The stories you love, set in exotic, glamorous locations...

HARLEQUIN PRESENTS,
Seduction and passion guaranteed!

Visit us at www.romance.net

HPGEN99

Harlequin® Historical

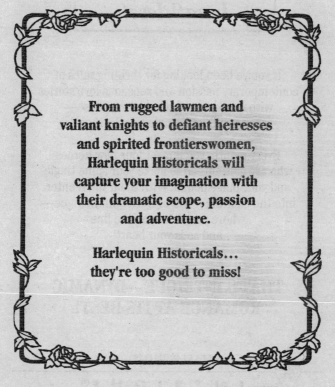

From rugged lawmen and
valiant knights to defiant heiresses
and spirited frontierswomen,
Harlequin Historicals will
capture your imagination with
their dramatic scope, passion
and adventure.

Harlequin Historicals...
they're too good to miss!

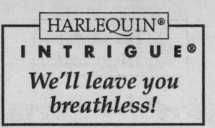